Born in Leicester, 1952, Spencer Coleman spent his early years near Portsmouth. He has been a successful artist in oils for over 30 years, working with Harrods and Danbury Mint, to name just a few companies. He is a member of the CWA and has published four novels and two short stories. This is his fifth suspense book. His print, *Bottoms Up*, was a big seller around the world. He likes snow-skiing and tennis. He has one son, who now runs the family gallery in Lincoln. In 2015, Spencer suffered a stroke but he is recovering well.

To Jordan and Molly, the best.

Spencer Coleman

THE SAFEST HIDING PLACE

AUSTIN MACAULEY PUBLISHERS™

LONDON • CAMBRIDGE • NEW YORK • SHARJAH

A CIP catalogue record for this title is available from the British Library.

ISBN 9781035823277 (Paperback)
ISBN 9781035823284 (ePub e-book)

www.austinmacauley.com

First Published 2023
Austin Macauley Publishers Ltd®
1 Canada Square
Canary Wharf
London
E14 5AA

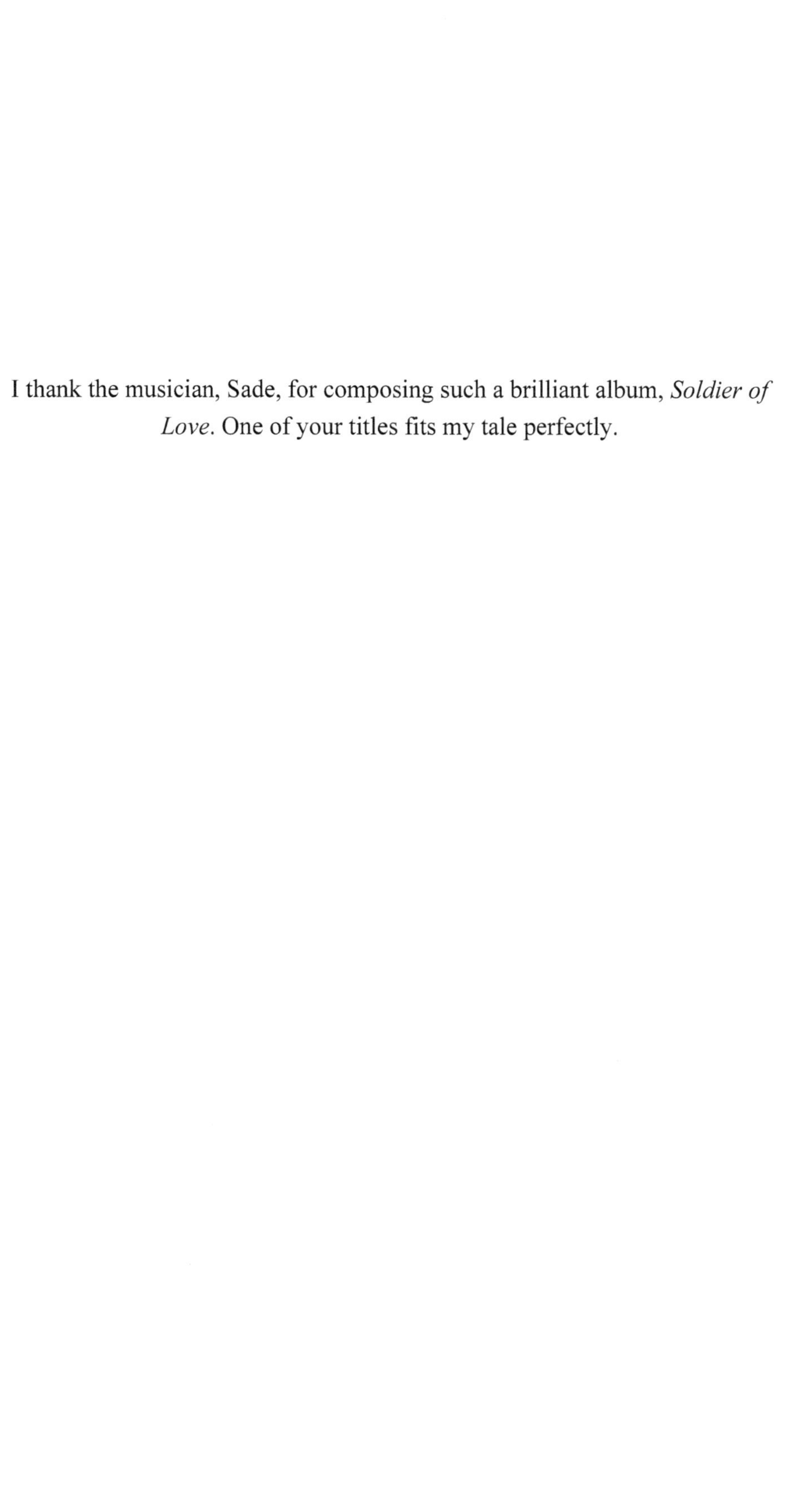

I thank the musician, Sade, for composing such a brilliant album, *Soldier of Love*. One of your titles fits my tale perfectly.

Chapter One

This is my fateful story but I didn't go to Venice on purpose to find it.

Instead, this sordid affair of my past found me unexpectedly on my international travels. My life seemed to turn upside down here, with what appeared like trivial events beyond my control suddenly hit me and soon became huge issues for my family to overcome. Could we? To do this, we had to painfully confront our perceived history. Not actually easy to do. People you love get hurt by this type of disclosure. Were we actually strong enough as a solid family unit back home in England to do this after I disclosed new information? After all, we had secrets like all people but these were best kept hidden from view to maintain harmony and the status quo to those affected by these heavy confessions. Well, that is my take on things in my current mood.

Maybe this would change. Watch this space if you dare. I watched this space, and it scared the hell out of me. But I am still me, warts and all. Oh dear.

There is trouble on the horizon. Always is, especially with me.

ooo

The winter song in any language is a barbed one and not for the faint-hearted; particularly for those of you in the throes of undying love and looking instead for a more lyrical prose, as you would expect in this most heavenly of settings. Actually, I prefer the darker and soulless lament, and I will pin my colours to the mast at the outset and confess that I'm not presently in love at the moment (ever the cynic, I tend to label this human sickness as blind devotion anyway in the direction of the opposite sex), so there you go. Rather, I am grappling with bitter divorce and all that it entails.

Many of you will know precisely what this means. It goes without saying therefore that, consumed by bitterness, I am in no position to give advice on misguided notions of eternal longings if Venice conjures up this image to you…which, indeed, it must of course, this being the home of Casanova and Byron, to name but two of the great romantics who made this their sexually-charged playground. So, I'm sorry that I'm just not the guy to endorse eternal love, not at this exact moment in time, because right now, I am in a bad place as far as relationships are concerned with women, as you would guess by my repetitive and pessimistic tone.

If you don't want me to spoil things and ruin your perception of what true happiness means for you, I suggest you listen instead to a summer sonnet and read Milton and quickly move on, leaving me to wallow in my own misery of events from the past, present, and the possible future. For those of stronger disposition, I can so easily burden you with my catalogue of marital failure, and no doubt I will if you stick with me. Two wives, two divorces: another on the way. I'm going for the hat-trick, but I certainly won't be celebrating this extraordinary feat like one of my goal scoring heroes, Robin Van Persie, would to his adoring fans as he stuck the ball in the net for the third time. (No, I'd rather keep a lower profile and hide in a darkened corner. I know my station in life.)

Ah, I soon hear you groan again at my alliance to this team called Manchester United. Yes, yes, for my sins I am a diehard red since my father took me to Old Trafford as a twelve-year-old, thirty odd years ago. In case I alienate you still further with other dubious proclamations, let's move on and bring you up to speed with my current situation. I should add that the first time I came to La Serenissima, I too was in love: blissfully so, as it happens. I mention that bloody word again. The word 'love' sticks in the brain.

That was many years ago though, and the girl who was my companion back then soon became my third wife. Her name is Lillian. We are now estranged and fighting custody of our dog, Bolly. Not an inspired introduction to bring you into my troubled world of mine (and present woes), but that's the sad imbalance of life and who said I was telling a fairy story anyway?

I once took part in Earnest Hemingway's challenge of concocting the definitive six-word storyline. My offering was *Blood on the door: successful exit.* I told you I was in a dark and, dare I say it, spiteful place.

Where there is divorce, there will be incriminations.

This tale is more than that though. My current existence could be described as a sinkhole into damnation. You don't have to stick with it if you are feeling a little queasy. But I suggest we start rather cautiously and see where it takes us, because it is a different kind of love that I aspire to, as you know already.

Am I giving too much away? This is more in line with duty, of loyalty and the strength of family unity. These things are important to me: they bring purpose to my life. Or so I am led to believe. Unfortunately, there are lies to contend with as well, which I will reveal later when I have had the chance to introduce to you the assembly of dubious characters that populate my mundane circle of friends and family members. Believe me, anything else thrown in at this early stage will just play havoc with your digestive system. I haven't even touched on my list of grievances of people and places as yet although I should mention that human betrayal is high on the agenda. My betrayal with the opposite sex, mainly. Let's take it one step further and really put the cat among the pigeons.

I have enemies, both in my private and professional life and they are ready to spill the beans as well. I will just get in first so there we go. They can always write a book and tell it how they see it.

It's probably a good idea even at this early stage to have a little breather at this point, make a cuppa, take things in, gather our wits about us, and reflect later on my dour preamble to a doomed relationship, which naturally points to flaws in my emotional make-up, I suppose. Ok, ok, I admit I am stuck in a disaster zone. Dunk a biscuit with your brew while you are at it, and snigger quietly to yourself. I can almost hear the collective muttering under your breath: *You don't say. Ha Ha!* If I laugh with you, we will end up crying together!

Hey, I'm searching for answers to many questions, so give me a little slack on this discovery. Then you can laugh or cry.

Why I am here in Venice? To find new artists for my exhibitions next year (as I am a gallery owner), or rather to escape my tortured mind and find solace in the poetic harmony of winding alleyways and hidden canals and crumbling facades, which in the latter case could accurately describe me. I am slowly falling apart, and so I feel at home here. No one can bear witness to the despair that is contained in my head, because I hide it so well, and I'm a stranger here, a tourist, which suits me as I go about my business quietly and methodically. Some hope, as you will find out shortly if you jump on this particular bandwagon. You have been warned.

I am also an artist of repute in the art world, and being here is also a reason to do my research for my upcoming exhibition called 'An Artist Abroad'. Also, I'm good at controlling people, hiding my pain and instead radiate my cool exterior in an outward manner which probably fools no one actually. So I suggest we follow my advice to slow the pace and meander the backstreets and examine the mysteries of this wondrous place together and slowly get to know one another, shall we? Well, I'll tell you my story first. Yours can wait until you decide to write about it as I have already explained. Are you an enemy of mine already?

Join the queue. There is no better beginning than the present, I believe. It stands to reason therefore that fearful reflection comes with the territory, so be prepared for the torrent of hurt that will inevitably follow in these pages. I am flawed, just like you. Sad, but true.

I liken my current circumstance to that first ripple of water which laps at your feet and then becomes the unsuspecting prelude to the tsunami racing in behind it. Be scared of the calm before the storm, my grandfather always used to say to me.

Chapter Two

So, we'll start with this simple scenario: Yours truly, adorning a long grey raincoat, standing as a solitary figure on a canal bridge, peering over and looking into the cold black water below and seeing my tortured soul as a reflection staring back at me, equally cold and equally black. It is not easy explaining my history, but I promise to tell the whole truth and nothing but the truth. Anything else is a smudged landscape, a quiet obsession painted badly by untrained hands. I am an artist, and so I know what to do with the brushes. I'll let you judge the merits of my oath as my story unfolds.

But I cannot speak for the others, of course, those who know me or those writing that damn book of theirs. I will try and give them a fair hearing, but I confess I will put myself in a good light in the hope that you will begin to like me. I am looking for validity in my life, an endorsement that I'm doing things the right way. I am a good man, an honourable man (you can be the judge of that statement!). On the flip side, if you were to ask one of my exes for their opinion then they might reply along the following lines: 'don't trust anything he says, now or forever'. So, believe what you want to believe. It has never harmed me, so make your own mind up. I explained earlier that I was flawed. First lie by me. I am not flawed, well, slightly. Well… you can decide if you read on. All my faculties are functioning (I hope!). But who then stated utter perfection existed in this world of ours? I didn't. Look elsewhere for the answer.

ooo

I check my watch and feel the hunger in the pit of my stomach. I move away from the bridge and stare in wonder at the architectural brilliance that surrounds me. Do I have to describe it to you? I doubt it. But this view takes some beating: Ahead, the majestic shape of The Church of the Santa Maria Della Salute looms heavy in the fog-shrouded landscape, the immense domes perched high above the structure below, which was elegantly bathed in a defused lemon sunlight. Gulls circle like floating handkerchiefs on the thermal airwaves.

The alleyway on which I stand is narrow and dark, and its insignificance makes me catch my breath as I marvel at the beguiling and grander beauty that presents itself from my modest vantage point, making me feel like a useless speck on the landscape. I button my raincoat up on this frosty late morning in early February. It is a sharp wind but I see a storm on the horizon so I am well prepared cloth-wise to any grim weather that greet me at this time of the year. All around, I am confronted by ochre-coloured ancient buildings and a darkly handsome people saturated in the beauty of poetry and paintings and sturdy monuments which miraculously adorn this great city in a rich symphony of Italian chaos.

From afar, I can hear the peel of church bells fracturing the bagel-scented air and feel at one with this place built so precariously upon thousands of Larch posts along the lacework of waterways…which are reminiscent to me of the thin gossamer threads which I observe from a spider weaving its intricate web under the archway above me.

I'm transfixed by this visionary beauty. Both the spider's work and the grandeur of my view.

Albert, my grandfather, who introduced me to this madhouse in the first place, calls Venice the Citadels on the Adriatic. He fought in Italy during the Second World War and returned many times since before ill health forced him to remain at home in care in England. Today, he is ninety-eight and has dementia. His son, Alec (my father), is showing early symptoms of the same disease at a sprightly seventy-five years of age. What chance for me to avoid the same prognosis, I ask? Let's not dwell on the same fate which probably awaits me. Happy days. Albert often joked (still does on a good day) that he had a dozen children living here, unbeknown to him. Fanciful I know, but he still remembers the names of all the pretty girls he chased during his numerous visits down the years, since his first encampment at the end of 1944. And who was I to argue with his joyous boasts? I rather enjoyed the stories actually.

They bring meaning to his drab existence of slow painful memory loss and the occasional memory gain of the pretty women who availed to the charms of new foreign men on their doorstep, this raises his spirits momentarily. Yes, he still brings up the name of a new Senorita every now and again! It is his birthday next month. I hope he makes it: he represents the last of a dying breed that fought and survived the war. Let us be grateful for their courage. There aren't many of them left to salute and give thanks to. I've digressed, as I am prone to do. My life by comparison is pedestrian. It's about to change. I should have stayed in London and wallowed in my historical ignorance.

I arrived earlier on a flight from Gatwick, checked into my rented apartment in the Cannaregio District near the Civil Ospedale (hospital) and sought solace from the winter chill by taking a tepid shower, and still the cold clung defiantly within my bones. I dressed quickly and tried cranking up the heating system but that too remained obstinate to my wishes of warmer water. I'm just grateful the maid carried out the owner's instructions and got the extra electricity switched on before my arrival. I soon took to walking the darkened pavements in search of coffee and cake, hoping that the pipes would gradually heat up and make things more bearable on my return to my temporary home which was a famous artist's place from London. This was a working studio, rather grand actually and cost a packet, I reckon.

But damn the expense of rental. If the divorce cost was going to wipe me out then better to spend the money now, before any solicitor got their grubby hands on it. Perhaps this trip was also not such a good idea of visiting other artists in order to nab their work for my own gallery to show as this also would cost me in the end. I don't want to pass on my bad mood to you. I see gloom in everything, and young lovers wrapped in each other's arms as they pass me hinder my mood further. I am cursed by my own shadow. I'm bound to cross a black cat, which is considered bad luck over here. I therefore tread carefully.

I eventually find a café down a narrow passageway, and weigh up my plight: I had taken refuge in this city on the pretext of a work related project, but in reality I was running away from my fucked-up thirteen-year marriage to Lillian. An unlucky number for some, certainly for me, and I am crushed under the weight of regret if I'm to be honest with you. I apologise profusely in advance for my morose character but I can't seem to rise above it, as I have already indicated to those of you patiently keeping up with me so far. Nor can the sporadic shafts of sunlight lancing through the solemn clouds lift my spirit either on this dismal day, it seems. The obstinate clouds cling low over the gothic city like a hand pressing heavy over my heart, but I take what comes my way. I still adore my wife, but it is easier to run away. Typical of a weak man. See, I avoided the word 'flawed', in case you hadn't noticed this.

So I sit and ponder the wisdom of my choice to come to a place like this: It is not for the clinically depressed, and really I should just do my job and pack my bag and leave. I'll cut you a deal and keep my thoughts to myself at the moment and not burden you with further talk of matrimonial discord. Instead, I prefer to sit here and drink myself into oblivion. Some of you will approve of this. I've gone off the idea of coffee. Jack Daniels seems preferable. I remain here for what seems an eternity, the empty bourbon glasses lined up like a firing squad to remind me of my guilt and sorrow. I know at some stage I'm going to be shot at dawn, metaphorically speaking of course. That's what happens when one becomes an ex-husband. Anyway, tomorrow is another day, so I'll have another drink: who's judging me anyway?

The good thing is you can't answer me back, which I'm grateful for.

I don't want counselling or words of wisdom. I think I just want to be left alone, adrift, unshackled for a while. I crave solitude.

It's not going to happen. There is always someone willing to talk about the weather, as the two dear ladies next to me do. Later, I move on and find another cafe-cum-pizzeria named Saraceno (just off the Rialto Bridge on the Riva Del Vin) which is empty of customers, but not for long. Fuck. An elderly man sits at the adjoining table; at first, we barely glance at each other as he unfolds a newspaper near me.

Had I looked more closely, I would have observed the devil in the detail and moved swiftly away from him. But I'm an innocent type, and take solace in alcohol once again and ignored him (or so I thought or hoped).

On reflection, I can pinpoint this exact moment as to how it all began, the prelude to my story. Unbeknown to us, maybe, we were two reluctant dancers waiting in anticipation for our fateful tune to commence. But we were hardly wallflowers in the music hall, as I was later to discover. We were obviously meant to meet each other at some point in our miserable lives. That juncture just happened to be right now. Weird but true.

Because I did stare back in his direction, and to my eternal damnation I was unaware of what was about to happen between us: that I was about to enter into a mutual contract of sorts so turbulent that in its silent malevolence I would be drawn into an unbeknown secret history which would bind us forever. One which my faltering spirit and crumbling heart could not contain, but still holds me captive every second of every day. I became cursed. I suppose being at my lowest ebb disabled my early warning system, because I didn't feel under threat by his presence. I would later call him a viper; but for now he was my compliant neighbour, with an easy charm and stories to tell. Had I looked closer, I would have seen the hidden ambition contained in his eyes, but at this moment in time

I was not the best monitor in matters of fairness and true character. I am going through a divorce. That should tell you everything about my nature. I'm flawed, ha ha, remember?

My big mistake, dear reader, was glancing upon his disfigured hand.

I tried to avert my gaze but you know how it is: The more you try to look away, the more intently you find yourself insensitively staring back: like we all do at a roadside car crash. The man's guarded reaction to this intrusion just added to my discomfort. It was not an ideal introduction, but it broke the ice I suppose when I eventually dared to catch his eye once again, moments later, without dropping my gaze this time. In the meantime, I played that peculiar British game of aloofness, hoping I hadn't offended him.

But I surely had.

We sat silently to begin with, my gaze now occupied by the industrial traffic on the Grand Canal outside. Sensing my crass behaviour, I then pretended to examine the sudden and rapid downpour of rain and sleet as it bounced off the exterior promenade: The choppy canal beyond quivered under a harsh sky of heavy grey wash, slashed by crimson stains which heralded the early lunchtime light.

The last of the gondolas bobbed on the swirling water, as the steersmen battled to find a safe haven beside the quayside, and no doubt swallow a welcome brandy in a nearby bar, like mine where I sat in comfort against the harsh elements as they beat down faster on the windows. I knew how they would be feeling and I felt queasy just watching their hard endeavours to tie up their boats in such difficult circumstances. I stared in horror as a wayward parasol suddenly tipped over outside, taking the table with it, causing broken glass to fly in all directions from discarded drinks left earlier. This wasn't a scene you would ever find in a glossy holiday brochure.

Soon, the dark cloak of the storm fell upon us, interrupted only by the line of twinkling decorative lights outside the restaurant showing a warm menu to visitors. The normally well-trodden promenade was largely deserted of tourists at this hour. Not surprising really. There was the odd idiot braving the elements, of course. Most sensible folk found shelter and warmth in their hotel or, like me, behind the protective window of a welcoming place of rest in order to escape the deluge like today. Mad dogs and an Englishman…blah, blah, blah!

Anyway, let's move on. I'll wager that you don't give a damn about the weather. You just want to know who the stranger is, right? Remember, I had found this place quite by chance which makes what follows decidedly unnerving. I usually behave myself in public but the disfigurement on show lured me in. It is difficult to avert one's gaze, idiot that I am. I repeat this scenario because I want to re-emphasise the unsettling nature of my bad behaviour and his gracious reaction to it.

Earlier, I had ordered another aperitif and up to then managed to keep my own counsel even though I was probably drunk from the Jack Daniels, not even conversing with the waiter, which I usually did to improve my elementary use of the Italian language. Now I had committed this *pas faux* and it was too late to hide the damage caused by my intrusive nature, much to my disgust.

So what did I do? You guessed it, I looked again.

In response to my curiosity, he raised his hand to the light from the chandelier hanging above from the ceiling, like it was a trophy of some kind. Well, it seemed so to my eyes anyway, but what did I know? I am referring to his hand, by the way, not the chandelier!

'A bullet wound from the war,' he announced in clear-clipped English behind a thick German accent.

Was my nationality that obvious to him? Then I remembered the Man United cap shoved tightly upon my head, another less notable trophy, compared to his proud boast.

'Bayern Munich,' he added with a thin smile as if in recognition to the allegiance to my own football team.

I mumbled these inept words, 'I'm sorry, I shouldn't have stared. It was rude of me.'

'There are a lot of unintentional rude people in the world,' he replied matter-of-factly.

I returned to my drink and fiddled with my camera as he ordered coffee in perfect Italian dialect and then spoke at length with an ease of confidence to the waiter, their banter punctuated with laughter. I was impressed by his confident linguistic skills.

Turning to me once again, he then asked: 'A Nikon twenty-seven?'

I looked up. 'You know about these things?'

'Like Marylyn Monroe, it is considered the perfect specimen, yes?'

I hadn't quite thought of it in those terms but I nodded my approval anyway. Obviously, my new friend liked weird comparisons.

'May I offer you a little something?' I suggested as a peace offering, raising my glass in his direction.

'Schnapps would be most agreeable…'

His coffee came and I got my order in, seemingly happy that I had atoned for my gross misconduct. I took the opportunity to study him in more detail.

His hair was thick and moon white and cut, like his clipped moustache, with precision. His eyes were cobalt blue, his jaw square and firm like a banister support. I guessed he was in his late eighties (older perhaps?), but his deportment was impressive: straight back, flat stomach, wide shoulders…all the hallmarks of a disciplined and proud ex-military man, I surmised. You could just tell. He reminded so much of how Albert, my uncle, sat upright. He then studied me. Not a lot to say, really. I was that ordinary. I felt stupid under his glare.

We remained silent until our drink arrived and then we toasted our brief union with a clink of glass.

'Helmut,' he announced.

'Martin,' I added.

We shook hands.

'I have a nephew by that name who works in London,' he said.

'Who with?'

'The *Deutsche* Bank near Liverpool street station,' he answered.

'How often do you visit him?'

'Oh, perhaps twice a year, if we are lucky.'

I'm on a roll with my new best friend and dig a little deeper. 'What brings you to Venice?'

'I'm signing copies of my latest book at a literary fair at the weekend.'

'A novel?'

'Part three of my memoirs…'

I'm impressed and intrigued and want to dig further: 'Is there a demand for such a thing in Italy?' I asked nervously.

He shrugs his shoulders with slight distain. 'Normally, none at all! But I am married to a very popular Italian TV presenter and that opens doors for me and buys me much needed publicity. We also own a home and a business here, and our daughter studies for her Degree in Rome.'

'You feel quite at ease then?' I asked. 'It is…how do you say…home from home. The Italians have adopted you.'

He laughs.

'Hardly. But it is something on those lines,' he said jovially. He took over the interrogation with an additional winning smile. 'They tolerate me is a more accurate description, because of whom I am married to. And you?'

'I'm doing research on new material for an art exhibition.'

'Are you an artist?'

'Artist and gallery owner…'

'Where are you based, my friend?' he asked, keeping the conversation flowing.

'London, on Cork Street, to be precise,' I replied.

He chuckled, and observed wryly: 'Expensive art then, eh?'

I nodded in agreement, enjoying his little aside remark.

'Perhaps on my next visit I will call in to see you,' he remarked.

I fumbled into my inside pocket and extracted a business card and passed it over.

He took it with his good hand and read aloud:

'Martin Snow Fine Art, specialising in British and European old masters. Hmm, very impressive for such a young man, may I say.'

'Not such a young man!' I protested, in a light-hearted manner. 'I took over the business from my father, who is now retired, so I don't take all the credit.'

He downed his Schnapps in one gulp. 'Are you buying paintings over here?'

'I'm here to organise this year's Christmas exhibition and I'm talking to a group of artists from this region, and I will headline it with my own work of this city. I hope to finalise the details and it is better for me to travel over here and meet with them face to face.'

'Easier to negotiate, I expect.'

I repeated his words in my head. 'Something like that,' I added loudly, warming to him.

'Which are you?'

'Pardon?'

'Old or a Master. Clearly British.'

I had to laugh again at his current observation. 'Neither, but my name helps pull in the punters!'

'Excellent, I do a little painting myself but not to the professional level that you would require. My work is more therapeutic as it allows me freedom to think when I've had enough of the word processor.'

The rain outside continued to detonate on the pavement as the heavens opened up, followed by the rumble of thunder high above. The crimson sky had been swallowed up by fast-moving predatory black clouds, which oddly resembled a division of panzer tanks rolling in unexpectedly. My imagination was getting the better of me. It must be because of my companion. The forks of lightning were reminiscent of big guns firing over the illuminated horizon.

I noticed that Helmut has a faint scar running diagonal across the length of his face. Although he smiled warmly, I detected a hint of cruelty behind the ancient Germanic features, particularly in the icy stare. I'm hooked enough though to carry on with the conversation. My voice became slightly deeper this time, me using a more authoritative tone in order to gain his friendship.

How needy was that?

He was about to speak, but we were suddenly interrupted by the vision of a vibrant woman who effortlessly glided in unannounced and, with familiar ease, joined us in the largely empty room, leant down and whispered in my companion's ear. Helmut slowly stood and hugged her, then turned to me: 'This is Sonia, my daughter.'

I stand as well and enthusiastically shake her hand, catching at once the fragility of her porcelain beauty and feline grace. She is not young; perhaps a couple of years off me, but is stunningly attractive. Her hair is black and long, her dress is black and sexy, her stockings and stiletto shoes are black. Her sculptured mouth is endorsed in glossy ruby red lipstick, matching her long alluring fingernails. I immediately want to record her smile with a click of my camera. I'm smitten, but I suppress my nervousness. I vow to not say something stupid in her presence, which would be typical of me. I hold the image of her face until even she is embarrassed and withdraws her hand from my clinging one. What was it with this family of strangers that I continually make a fool of myself?

Her father seems to explain in his native dialect who I am (he is pointing at me) while I remain faithfully dumbstruck. She eventually tilts her head in my direction, nods, and then takes his arm gently and leads him towards the exit.

'We are late for the Opera,' he shouts in my direction. At the revolving door he turns again and bellows, 'War! That is all I know…'

I wave in acknowledgment; then they are gone. I am feeling a little dumbstruck to be honest. I finish my drink with one swallow. As I leave, somewhat giddy with desire, I see a poster on the wall in the small vestibule by the revolving doors. I can easily translate it:

An evening seminar with Helmut Grohmann

Saturday, 22nd February 2014, 7pm
The esteemed war veteran, politician and author will be reading from his lates memoir, followed by a Q&A with the audience.
Signed copies of 'At War with Myself' will be available at a special preview price.
Book now. Limited seats available.
Venue: University Reading Room.

I check the rest of the details and tap them into my mobile: the venue is the prestigious university and I note the address and phone number.

I decide on the spur of the moment to attend, hoping at the very least to engage Sonia in conversation this time, if I'm lucky enough to meet her again.

Returning to my apartment, I discard my hat and raincoat, eat modestly by whipping up an omelette of ham and mushrooms, washed down with a glass of orange juice, which I had purchased earlier from the local supermarket. I was done with alcohol (for now!). The heating has gathered momentum and I was able to remove my sweater and roll my shirtsleeves up.

I took stock of my temporary home. It was a huge size and must have cost a fortune, and would be described as a *mansarda,* in reference to living in the roof space. Some roof space! The open plan living area was divided up into one third art studio, one third living area and one third kitchen, which was ultra-sleek and looked like it had never been used. Except by me.

The apartment didn't have views of the canals, which probably reduced the financial outlay somewhat, but, hell, it was still mightily impressive. It was originally a plumber's merchants house, used for storage, I later learned.

There was a mezzanine floor at one end which contained a master bedroom and a further bedroom and bathroom at the rear, which contained a Jacuzzi and sauna. The paintings adorning the walls were by the celebrated artist himself, a certain Norman Neville RA and were a mixture of figurative and landscape in oils. Three of the canvasses were of Venice. The work was assured and dynamic, as you would expect from a Royal Academician no less.

The furniture was a mix of antique and modern, thrown together with accomplished ease. Rather chaotic but classy all the same. I felt at home.

Chaotic described me.

I checked my mobile and discovered I had a missed call from Lillian. I was in no hurry to report back to her. Any conversation between us would end in tears on her part, as we usually argued over divorce money.

Instead, I made myself comfortable and booted up my laptop and googled the biographical details of my esteemed German companion at the pizzeria.

There was a lot to digest, which soon forced me to uncork a bottle of red wine.

My willpower is sadly lacking in this department. I settled down in one of the white squidgy sofas and kicked off my shoes, content with the calmness of my surroundings. No one can get me here, I thought. I begin to absorb the weighty text which unfolded on my Apple and realised my new acquaintance was famous in the Second World War as well as a best-selling writer, when the doorbell rang unexpectedly, disturbing my train of thought. Damn the intrusion. Just when I was settled and engrossed with my reading.

I was annoyed at the enforced noise and chose to ignore it. It doesn't ignore me and persists, my irritation intensifying with each electronic gong. Whoever it is, it is evident they are not going away, and the light at my window suggests someone is at home to this intruder. There is no escape for me.

Reluctantly, I open the heavy oak door down below at street level and I'm confronted by a dishevelled man, clearly pissed and holding a bottle of cognac, accompanied by a girl clinging to him in order to stay upright. She is giggling; he is looking me up and down in obvious discord.

'Who are you?' the stranger on the doorstep asks, slurring his words.

'Who are you?' I repeat sharply. I'm baffled by this interruption.

He ignores me and gently sways with this girl on wobbly legs, her heaving breasts suddenly on view. I would say she is perhaps twenty, he may be twice as old. I can smell the alcohol on them. He persists, looking wide-eyed beyond me: 'Where is…the…old fella?' he hollers. The man pushes past me, shouting wildly again, 'Norman? Norman?'

I'm agitated. 'Norman isn't here,' I protest, following the stranger up the stairs and grabbing his arm. By now the girl has entered too, flopping down on one of the sofas after stumbling up after us.

'I suggest you leave,' I demand.

He turns and pulls away from my grip, almost spitting the words: 'Chill, man!' in my direction.

I'm in no mood for this pair of unwanted guests. 'Look, Norman will be over next week…I'm here alone, I've rented this house to be alone at great expense. How about you call him then?'

The man takes a gulp of his firewater and looks me up and down, and introduces himself with this unwelcome comment: 'I need a piss.'

I begin to protest still further and say, 'Look, how about…'

I'm brushed aside as the man rudely saunters off to the rear of the building in search of a loo. I hope he finds it! He looks like he could turn mean, so I make a decision to cool it and humour them. Even though the cold is creeping in, I deliberately leave the door open to the street, aware that people are ambling past in case I need their urgent assistance. The girl appears to be asleep already, sprawled on the sofa.

I knock back my glass of wine and do a quick refill. I swivel on my heels as the stranger returns, zipping up his fly and knocking into a table. This confirmed to me he was drunk as he was close to being.

'Jack,' he announces with a thump of the chest and shakes my hand. Then he points to the stricken girl. 'And this is Jill…'

I laugh nervously. Before I put two and two together, he lets out an uproarious laugh and bellows: 'Just like in the song, man!'

'Martin Snow,' I reply by way of an introduction, but I decline to shake his hand again. 'Hey, I've flown in today and I need to sleep. Any friend of Norman's is a friend of mine, but can we do this tomorrow, Jack?'

I silently move to the door down the stairs and widen it still further.

He hesitates, burps and nudges his girl with an outstretched boot.

'Come on, Jill, seems we're not welcome here…'

She stirs and he lifts her to her feet, but I'm only worried that she doesn't suddenly throw up over the expensive looking rug we are standing on. I don't care that my manners are rude. I want rid of them. To his credit, Jack drags her to the street, shouting back at me as they stagger into the night, 'See you around, man!'

I shout my name again but to no avail, and I quickly close the door and bolt it, convinced I have seen the last of them during my stay. I'm suddenly restless and finish the bottle of wine and notice, to my horror, that Jill has forgotten her shoulder bag which lay discarded on the floor, some of the contents scattered around it.

Fuck, I wasn't going out in the cold to search for them down the narrow walkways. I put coffee on and knew that I would indeed be making their acquaintance again, sooner than I wished for, to be honest. As I repacked her things, I couldn't help but notice that contained within the bag was an invitation to Helmut Grohmann's seminar on the forthcoming Saturday night. I could only hope that my new best friends would be sober on the evening in question, or it could be a calamitous event.

I went to bed with a real feeling of foreboding swilling around in my gut.

ooo

Mellow light filtered through the skylight and disturbed my fitful dreams.

My mouth was dry from the wine the night before so I stumbled to the kitchen, gulping water from the tap. I found it difficult adapting to my new home. It was too big for me. I had booked it at the last minute, taking advantage of a cancellation (although I didn't get a discount, much to my disgust) so I shouldn't really complain at the size of the place. My first though was that the artist was obviously doing rather well financially, owning a substantial property in Venice, although it was situated in a less celebrated area called Fondamenta Nuove, more like a working quarter of the Cannaregio District and therefore cheaper than overlooking The Grand Canal which would cost a packet.

The entire interior ceiling was heavy with massive wooden beams, which seemed to press down on my head and shoulders, adding to my already troubled conscience. That aside, I was naturally fascinated by the studio, which smelled of linseed oil and contained a mass of paint pots and brushes and dominated by three huge easels. A pile of unused primed canvasses were stacked against a wonderful old plan chest. Norman's art collection, dotted around the walls, was impressive I had to admit too. I had never represented him, or sold his work down the years and he was now managed exclusively by a London agent in Mayfair. I was small fry in comparison.

I washed and dressed and, using the map at my disposal which I got at the airport, found a better supermarket than the first one I tried and stocked up with essential foods. I plated up smoked salmon and scrambled eggs and brewed coffee, ready for the day ahead. Checking my itinerary for the next few days, the first appointment was in the afternoon at a gallery behind the Academia Bridge, near the Guggenheim Museum. I had done business with this gallery before, and three of their artists appealed to me. There was negotiation to be done.

Although I had visited the Guggenheim Museum before, I was a sucker for punishment and decided to cast my critical eye over the collection once again.

There was always something here to surprise the onlooker (and allow me the chance to dishonour Picasso once again, as I can't stand his work) and a new exhibition at the venue, running for just another week, enticed my senses so it seemed an obvious decision to pop in whilst I was in the vicinity. Besides, I loved the exhibits in the Nasher sculpture garden, particularly the Henry Moore bronze entitled 'Working model for Oval with Points.' I walked the narrow alleyways, camera in hand, taking snaps of the waterways and architecture which hopefully I could use myself for future paintings. The light remained good and I felt elated by the visual discoveries that greeted me at each turn on my journey. My camera came to good use and justified its expense. Thankfully, I had put my two strange acquaintances at my apartment from the day before to the back of my mind, although I had left a thoughtful message on the door explaining my absence. I knew the girl would be anxious to retrieve her handbag, but I wasn't going to disrupt my day in the assumption she might turn up. I had noticed she did have a good arse, so to be fair something exciting would come of it eventually I hoped. Some hope, but you can dream. It cost nothing.

After stopping for coffee in a nearby cafe, I reached the Museum an hour later and much to my surprise, and utter delight, I spotted Sonia ahead of me in the admission queue. My heart raced at this discovery. I decided to hold back from introducing myself, preferring to observe her (rather like an exhibit, much to my shame) from a safe distance. I was, as you can guess, besotted by this heavenly creature. In truth, I was terrified of making a complete prat of myself by opening my mouth and saying something utterly inappropriate. It wasn't long though before she spotted me inside the museum skulking in a corner and came over, while I pretended to be enthralled by a tasteless Miro in front of me.

'It's Martin, isn't it?' she asked.

I turned with a slightly bemused look on my face.

'Yes…' I said in a confused tone. I was good at this playful game. Told you I was controlling! It didn't surprise me. Just act dumb, and the rest will follow naturally. I knew how to impress folk. Ok, have a laugh.

'You were with my father yesterday,' she stated.

'Yes.'

She cocked her head. 'Is that all you can say?'

'Well…' I stopped myself just in time. I couldn't keep this charade going forever. 'Was the opera good?' I asked pathetically.

'Divine.' She waved her arms wildly. 'Are you a fan of this collection?'

'Indeed.'

She pressed on, trying to get further enthusiasm from my inadequate responses. 'Which is your favourite piece?'

That stumped me, and then I blurted out: 'I rather like *Empire of Light* by Rene Magritte.'

She smiled warmly and added excitedly, 'That is my favourite piece too!'

I suddenly felt elated and my shoulders immediately straightened.

Sonia took my arm and squeezed reassuringly, insisting: 'What makes it so special for you?'

My shoulders quickly slumped, and then, as if by some miracle, I remembered the blurb written on the label next to the painting and tried to sound half-intelligent. It was my job after all. But I somehow struggled in her company. I cleared my faltering throat. 'Well, it is both the surprise and enchantment contained within the scene with the lack of narrative, which also conjures up imminent drama by the blackness of night, the absence of people and the two lights on behind the windows to the side, which makes it all a bit spooky. We search for something that isn't there.' God, that was impressive and supposedly spoken off the cuff. Had she twigged me?

'Exactly!' She takes my arm and escorts me to the work in question. I obviously got away with it. We stare at the picture in silence, although secretly I have dirty thoughts designed on my companion. I remain calm, and smell her delicate perfume as it lingers in the air. She whispers, 'It is almost exotic, don't you think?'

I panic, wondering if she can read my mind.

'It is serene and threatening,' I say, which is exactly how I feel; and I want the ground to swallow me up. But then I will lose her, so I spurt out the only thing which seemed appropriate: 'Would you like coffee before seeing the rest of the exhibits?'

'That would be perfect,' she replies alluringly, her sexy expression suddenly pulling me in.

I've scored, and almost punch the air in triumph. I lead her away from the label. I bet at this precise moment you are having a little wager to yourself, wanting to proclaim with smug satisfaction that she is way out of my league.

Perhaps so, but she didn't turn my offer down, did she, wise-ass? And this was romantic Venice after all. The city for lovers, as Albert always told me, even though inside my body, I felt morose. Who was I to doubt the great man at a moment like this? The timing seemed perfect and perked me up no end. Simple things cheered me up. How about you?

ooo

I had concluded my business with the gallery owner (he bought forward our appointment) earlier and secured the services of the three artists I was interested in, and in return I will supply work from my end on a reciprocal basis. This helped to promote and widen the international market for all concerned. I'm more than happy but the real elation lies with my fortuitous chance encounter with Sonia, a woman to gladden the heart of any man.

Over coffee, we engaged in the usual small talk that dictates such occasions, but I did learn that she too was going through recent divorce procedures, and was accompanying her father in order to distract herself from further emotional strife from being too near the battlefield at home. I knew the feeling only too well. I refrained at this stage to burden her with my complex story for fear of frightening her away, but I did explain my predicament in the simplest of terms and moved on, preferring to talk art and the history of Venice, which I know something about. After three failed marriages, I couldn't profess to know anything about the complexities of the opposite sex…and wanted to avoid the subject altogether for fear of embarrassing myself further.

Changing the subject smoothly, I asked after her father. She informed me that he was resting at home on the Islands after the night of entertainment, and was anxious that his wife was feeling a little unwell in Munich. She was undergoing medical supervision and was unable to travel to her home country.

Because of professional commitments, he felt obligated to attend to such matters which in turn made leaving her all the more difficult. But they coped, and her ailments were not life-threatening.

Sonia surprised me by suggesting that we meet up for dinner one evening, as her and her father had taken an apparent liking to me. I was hardly going to turn such an invitation down (and miss the chance to see her again), but I protested anyway because we were in essence complete strangers and I would have felt like an intruder in the circumstances. She in turn brushed my concerns away and insisted on the Friday evening, if I was free, of course. Ha, I pretended to check my mobile phone and, not surprisingly, discovered that I was indeed free that night.

We had a date for 8 pm in the Grill at the Gritti Palace Hotel on San Marco. I wasn't one to complain. Further proof, I hasten to add to those wayward folk that continue to scoff, that I was winning her over with my natural charm and exceedingly good looks. I'm allowed to gloat on a few rare occasions. Take it on the chin, you sceptics!

When I got back to the apartment on Ramo E Corte Del Paludo, I barely had time to kick my shoes off when the knock on the door warned me of the most unwelcome of visitors, but I vowed to keep civil in the hope that my only task was to hand over a handbag. Nothing is ever that simple.

'We called earlier,' Jack announced, pushing past me with Jill in tow, who hardly growled in my direction. She looked like a zombie. Her reddened eyes suggested a night and day of continued boozing.

I tracked down the bag and handed it over to her, but I got no thanks in return. 'Glad to be of help,' I offered meekly, moving back towards the half-opened door to the street.

Jack stared me down. 'The old man said we could use his studio to paint.'

'Oh?' I was naturally taken aback. He appeared threatening with his stance.

'I phoned him last night, to check first,' Jack informed me.

'Well, he hasn't spoken with me. I thought I had the place exclusively…'

'You've been out most of the day. Have you listened to the answer-machine?'

I hadn't.

'Norman often allows me to set up on his easels, especially if I have a deadline to meet.'

This was becoming a stand-off.

'And you have a deadline to meet, I assume?'

'That about sums it up…'

Jill sat down on the sofa and fiddled with her bag.

'How long will you be?' I asked pointedly, standing my ground.

'If tomorrow is OK….The full day should do it, man.'

My heart sunk at his words. I was in no position to decline him as Norman's say-so was gospel to colleagues in this region. I was not a colleague, just a punter. The lowest of the low, it appeared.

Chapter Three

That night I ate out alone at a local restaurant and planned a day away from the studio tomorrow and allow my "guest", Jack, time uninterrupted in the hope he would finish before nightfall. That was the plan. I had sketching to do anyway, or pursue camerawork if the weather changed for more rain.

I returned Lillian's call with all the enthusiasm I could muster but my mind was on another woman…and her name was not Jill in case you were wondering. I'm not that shallow, am I? Don't answer that!

'Hi,' I said cautiously. 'Just returning your message. You want me?'

I listen to her rant as I devour the spaghetti in front of me. To any random onlooker, I am Mr Cool personified but under the skin I am seething but I keep externally calm even though I am being stared at by other diners now. They have no idea of how I feel, unless they can work out my abusive English lingo on top of an assassin's smile. I told you I can mask my true feelings, but customers were beginning to see through this polite façade. I am not that good an actor. Besides, I cannot keep to a script! First rule of bitter divorce: You can run but you can't hide, I learnt to my cost.

'Where are you anyway?' she asks down the phone.

'Venice,' I mutter.

'For how long?'

'For a few days, maybe a week.'

'All right for some!' She snaps.

I finish our conversation abruptly. 'I am here doing research for my new show, which incidentally helps pay you and your solicitor. Ok darling, do what you want in the morning. Just remember I hate your fucking guts, you morose idiot, so let the best man win.' With that, I click off my mobile and order a second glass of wine, much to the waiter's amusement at my awkward stance on the matter. I must control my temper. The waiter must also know English.

I wish I could share in his laughter but the spaghetti was good and comforting on this cold night and I concentrated on this. It strangely placated me. Fuck her, she had a valid point but she was interfering with my meal. I was over the top with my last rant. I prioritise everything wrongly. It is what men do, rather badly, most of the time. Will we ever learn? It is described as the battle of the sexes.

I get back to my rented abode, have another shower and retire for the night, ready for an early start and an interruption from yours truly…you know who I am referring to. The so-called artist.

Yep, you guessed it. Jack surprisingly arrived at eight o'clock and set up at one of the easels hardly saying a word except "Good morning". He surprisingly appeared sober. My offer of a hot drink was met by a grunt.

Overall, I was impressed by his early arrival and even made him a black coffee (no alcohol, you notice). He shrugged indifferently at this gesture of mine. I just wanted to start the day properly for him but I made sure I kept all my credit cards and cash on me just in case. You never know with a stranger in your midst and I wasn't prepared for my clothes to be rifled while I was away for the day. Well, what would you do in the same circumstances?

I bid my farewell and told him I would return at six, and I expected an empty studio. Some hope of mine!

He shrugged his shoulders again at this remark and somehow I knew my designated return would not be welcomed by my guest.

'Six o'clock,' I re-emphasise on my way out but I was talking to a deaf man, I reckon. He mumbled something like he would be finished when he was finished.

I did the only response I could think of: I shrugged my shoulders.

ooo

Taking the water taxi, I headed for the island called Giudecca where I was informed a famous artist lived and worked. I had never been to this place before and spent two hours exploring the waterfronts and back alleys, and sketching, until having a refreshing drink at the plush Hilton Hotel on one side of the Island overlooking the city across the wide main canal. I visited the artist, Godfrey Snapp, at his palace at our appointment for midday. He was like royalty over here and I felt out of my depth. But who cares? He could only say "No" to my request of an exhibition. It was only a two-minute stroll from the Hilton and it was easy to find, although a large house described it better than a palace.

Either way, I was equally impressed. He was a Londoner by birth, elderly and charming to be in his illustrious company for the hour I was allotted before

32

his next sitting. He was a figurative artist and very well known in Venice and beyond, specialising in female nudes among other things. Godfrey showed me his small drawings and interior still life paintings and we toured the house itself which was huge…. perhaps a palace was appropriate after all and then we went to his studio at the front overlooking the water.

The studio space which was full of light and the partition wall was glass rendered which gave the artist greater scope to depict his model. In the middle was his easel and further props for his sitter. I was so engrossed I walked past a nude model. Her youth and nakedness was on display but I swear she never budged her erotic posture except for a polite "hello" in my direction. Shocked, I mumbled the same greeting to the accented American girl and averted my eyes to the framed masterpieces on the walls. Wow, was I impressed by Godfrey's talent and the company he kept! I had clearly interrupted his work, despite my appointment.

'Tea or coffee?' he asked me, moving towards the kitchen. 'And you can get dressed, Mia. Our session is over.'

I shouted "coffee" to his back while my gaze was affixed to the pile of unfinished canvases as Mia got dressed behind me. I caught a glimpse of her voluptuous reflection in the mirror. No wonder his pictures were mainly incomplete as the next heavenly creature would turn up for a private session of his!

I recovered my composure and got down to business as he found a tray nearby and loaded it with just two cups and saucers and biscuits and a sugar bowl. My thoughts were interrupted by his sudden arrival in the studio from the kitchen, I gathered. A pity as I was taking a shine to his sitter and I spoke fluent American. What could possibly go wrong? But back to business which you really want to hear about. Yes? I thought not! Don't steal my fantasies.

That is all I have at present, so leave them to me, please. Yes, I know I am pathetic! We have already touched on this subject!

'When did you last exhibit in England?' I enquired of him as Mia departed the building with a curt farewell and a wave. I would miss her and her divine body!

Godfrey ignores her and says to me directly, 'Twenty odd years ago.'

I'm stunned by this, but react positively, 'Then let me offer you a One man show next May.'

'No, thank you.'

'Is there a reason for this decision?' I'm baffled by his response.

'Because of commitments, a lack of new work for you and…I don't need the hassle.'

'From me?'

'I do my own thing. It suits me. Besides, I don't want to paint new work exclusively to you. I have my own gallery here in Venice on the main Island and that keeps me busy.'

'No need to paint new work.' I thought quickly. 'When was this work (I waved my arm at his storeroom) ever shown in London?'

'It hasn't.'

'Exactly, let me pick from your vast stock and you do not need to do a thing. It will be a major success.' I was excited by this opportunity and hoped he would as well. What a coup for me! I could even smell the money from the resultant big sales.

'I'll think about it, but a firm no still commands my decision.'

This was as good as it got. I studied his unsold work further, drank my coffee, and then my hour was up. How time flies! I thanked him for his hospitality and vowed to return. He nodded and showed me the front door down a flight of steps. Hmm, my persuasive tongue was failing me.

Just then, to my utter amazement, Sonia turned up and said 'hello' to me.

'Do you know one another?' Godfrey asked on the street.

'We do indeed,' I uttered, thinking of her naked body he would soon be staring at. Some people get all the best jobs.

'A portrait, in case you were wondering, with no nudity,' she added quickly, before my mind goes into overdrive like yours. 'We are having dinner together,' Sonia says to the artist on his doorstep. She points to me, before slipping up the stairs.

'Do you know Helmut?' Godfrey asked me.

I nod.

'Well, any friend of his is a friend of mine. Shall we get together tomorrow at eleven in the morning for a proper drink?'

I nodded my approval. I was making new friends by the hour.

I owed Helmut a big toast if he helped my newfound influence on artists too grand for my gallery back home, and my newfound status as a nearly single man. Watch it, Sonia. Then I was gone (with my vivid, over the top, imagination). Which always spelled trouble on the horizon wherever my footsteps took me.

I spent the rest of the afternoon visiting galleries and found two new artists who would fit neatly into my mixed shows but I really hoped for the One man exhibition by Godfrey Snapp for May, as it would surely be a steal for me and make me a serious player in the rarefied world of Fine Art, especially in London. And I was one step ahead of any competitor in the game. What a coup that would be if I could get him!

At just past six I returned apprehensively to the apartment and found Jack thankfully packing up and leaving the studio. Boy, was I relieved but an inspection of his work I discovered he was rather good. so I lingered over the finished canvasses. He was taking this opportunity to subtly improve twenty odd local views for his solo show in the Cotswold which I remarked should do well if this was a selection of what to expect. I thought I was being supportive but he simply shrugged and mumbled something under his breath…what he said I didn't get and I didn't ask him to repeat it for fear of a further long conversation and my evening, therefore, possibly ruined. I wasn't prepared for that, just happy that Jack brought on board my morning instructions which he adhered to. I was grateful, and he remained sober as well. Miracles do happen!

Jill made coffee for all of us and for the first time I had a chance to look them over as a couple. They were a good-looking pair, he a tall lean specimen adorned in blue denim with long blondish hair and the roguish looks of an artist; she of the pert arse was equally tall wearing all white blouse and jeans, with a smile to cause a car crash. Quite simply, Jill was ravishing with dark brown eyes under a red-haired bob. She lit up a cigarette and I was instantly hooked but I knew she only had those eyes for him. Lucky bugger, I thought, and turned my attention to my forthcoming meal at the Hotel Gritti.

That promised to be fun, or so I hoped!

'Thanks,' offered Jack, as I helped them fill their backpacks to the brim and carted everything to the front door. I bade them farewell, then shaved, cleaned my teeth and took my first proper hot shower, which was bliss. As I dressed, my body was devoured by the heating system which had warmed the vast space admirably. I was grateful for this. I felt somehow renewed.

I strolled the back streets and waterways and shops and it took about twenty minutes to reach the Hotel Gritti overlooking the vast expanse of water. The crowds were out on this unseasonably balmy evening (thank God the rain had gone) and I cut through them with ease across St Mark's Square. I studied the Bridge of Sighs from my vantage point. This view never bored the senses, it was magical watching lovers take the gondolas on a trip under the stars and across the lagoon. The Salute shimmered in the distance and little lights on the wide promenade beneath my feet flickered on giving this February a certain Christmas "feel". People loved this, coupled with the Carnival activity at this time of year. It was what Venice was all about for tourists. Intoxicating.

At the Hotel entrance I am met by three gorgeous girls dressed in long silk gowns and masks and a horde of photographers surrounding them like bees to the honey. I am a sucker for this type of thing and get my picture taken with them. You only live once.

Eventually, a waiter rescues me (whoever told him I needed rescuing?) but Helmut and Sonia are waiting for me impatiently at our candlelit dining table.

'I was rather hoping we were eating alone,' I whispered to Sonia, sitting down rather too quickly at our plush darkened position. The restaurant was busy.

'That's the deal. Daddy insisted on joining us, and I couldn't say no.'

'Is there a problem?' said Helmut. 'The Press have been sniffing around the house and we just want to eat in peace. This probably was not the right place.'

'Suits me,' I say. 'By the way Sonia, you look beautiful tonight.' I kissed her hand gently and added, 'not that you don't look beautiful all the time.'

'Thank you. And you look good as well.' She beamed.

My last remark just got me out of jail and we all seemed to relax. I admonished myself silently. Don't whisper behind my back, dear reader. I have thick skin. Believe what you want to believe! I am here, you are not, so any compliment from Sonia is very welcome to me. In fact, it makes me feel great. And she invited me to meet for dinner, not the other way around.

Bingo!

'How's your portrait going?' I enquired.

'By Godfrey…?'

'Costing…how you say…a packet,' Helmut cursed, looking at me.

I laugh, then added, '…worth every penny.'

Sonia beams still further at me, which puts me into seventh heaven.

'If only we were talking pennies,' Helmut says with a grin and then takes his daughter's hand and squeezes it reassuringly. 'There is no one else. Godfrey is the best and the best don't come cheap.'

'That is an English term,' I observe, referring to the use of the word 'pennies'.

'Old habits die hard,' Helmut recollected. I nod approval and work out a fee of twenty thousand euros. I gulp at this amount. The drinks waiter came to our table from nowhere again and we order an aperitif: gin and tonics all around. This stops us discussing money. I feel we are all grateful for that.

We eat in silence, and my medium rare fillet steak is excellent. Helmut has the same as me and Sonia settles on grilled tuna. We share a salad and a bottle of Argentinian Malbec. It is a good evening only interrupted by two autograph hunters asking for Helmut's signature. He duly obliges with a courtesy as you would expect but any press reporter was given 'short shrift' for digging for any gossip on his wife's illness. I was not asked for my scrawl. In fact, I was ignored. Oh, how the other half live!

Over coffee, we discussed football and other pointless subjects and conclude the national champions as Bayern Munich and Chelsea (ugh, I hear you groan, at our obvious choices after an intense hour of debate). Sonia agreed with a yawn but Helmut was enthralled with my mundane knowledge of German football. A pity his divine daughter didn't share the same enthusiasm as us. Her yawn was followed by another yawn.

I change the subject and speak at no one in particular. 'How do you know Godfrey?'

Her eyes light up at this remark and I know I have her attention once more, which thrills me.

Helmut knocks back his second black coffee and pours another one while I wait and take an opinion on Sonia. She is wearing a backless red dress and her flawless skin is playing havoc with my hormones. Her hair is glossy black, and tied up at the top on her head by way of a diamond encrusted clasp. She is truly beautiful and I am captivated by her high cheekbones, expressive 'come to bed' eyes, her wide mouth and a cleavage to happily die in. Wow, what a package and suddenly I was jealous of the artist in question.

'Ah, Godfrey and I go back many years and I like to think my early purchases helped put him on the map when he first came to Venice,' Helmut duly remarked, hijacking the story with his interruption and ruining my fantasies.

'And when was that?' Sonia said, beating me to the obvious question.

'In the late sixties, thinking about it,' Helmut said.

'And does that include those paintings at home?' She asked with a winning smile in the direction of her father.

Damn, I was now envious of Godfrey. I had to think of something clever to say to get her attention again. I fail miserably and can't think of anything witty to say to accomplish this thought.

'I reckon we have sixty altogether, or more!' Helmut laughed like a man just diagnosed with terminal cancer as he started counting. 'He must have been grateful at such an early patronage and you get the lot in the end, Sonia. Assuming, of course, that you are the only heir.'

'I am,' she shrieked.

'She is, I think,' he said in the same breath, laughing this time.

'You are a tease, Daddy.'

'A fair sum,' I said quietly on reflection of his admission to the quantity mentioned.

'Some of them were cheap, but it helped him get established,' Helmut yelled above the din of the other sitters. Gazing around, I saw one or two celebrities nearby. I was impressed to be in their company.

'Money is money,' I said, holding my hands up.

'Exactly. What are you doing tomorrow?' he asks.

'Apart from coming to your book signing in the evening and seeing Godfrey late morning, I have the afternoon free,' I said. 'I was going to do some extra sketching, but this can be put off.'

'Excellent. I am rehearsing for the show from ten for two hours then I am free. Shall we meet up?'

I begin my artificial protest.

'That's settled then, I'll meet you on the Academia Bridge at one o'clock. I'll show you my Venice.' He stood. 'What are you doing, my dear?'

She took his arm. 'I'm seeing Godfrey for a sitting again.'

I looked at her and my insides suddenly died at this news. It was like a stake through the heart.

ooo

It was great to have Norman's house to myself but I dreamt about the thought of Sonia with me so there you go. My imagination getting the better of me again but you can hope it will happen! Dreams are free.

Anyway, I slept well and made breakfast in the morning of scrambled eggs on toast and slowly made my way by water taxi to Giudecca for eleven as planned. I was surprised to find Godfrey waiting for me by the front door.

'Hello,' he announced, as a stranger walking past shook his hand and whispered something cordial by the look of artist's smile in response.

'Hello.' I shook his hand. 'Nice to be famous,' I observed.

'It can be useful, but I have been here over forty years so I expect certain civilities. I am a local after all. Fame goes with the territory…but I have earned my success. I work hard although it doesn't seem I do to certain people!'

I nod my approval. How do you respond to that kind of remark?

'Just going to my art shop…thought you might like to see it,' Godfrey said.

'Yes please,' I added obediently as we caught the next water taxi and headed in the direction I had just come from. So I was well pissed off as it cost me again. I should have bought a day pass. I was delighted with his wisdom on our travels and learnt about the slave trade and the affect it had on the area as we crossed the canal. He was well-informed. I just listened. We settled on the Dorsoduro district and arrived at our first destination called Cantine del Vino Gia Shrive. No art shop in sight! What a surprise, I thought, but ran with his misleading observation. Beggars can't be choosers! I felt like a beggar in the circumstances.

'One of the oldest wine bars in the region,' he said, 'and my local,' he added mischievously. He then whispered in my ear, 'just keep our visit quiet from my wife if you meet her!'

My lips were sealed! It was going to be a long session. We ordered the local red wine and had food and ate at the counter like most of the other customers. I felt at home in his world of strangers to me. Most said 'hello' or patted Godfrey's back in some sort of recognition of his presence. I was ignored in his company but still felt like a King being his esteemed guest on this occasion. We drank again as he regaled on old funny stories as nearby listeners laughed and clapped at his punch line and I laughed dutifully even though he spoke in the local lingo and I didn't understand the joke. It was the least I could do, being civil on his patch. I offered to pay at the bar but my protests were easily knocked back by the staff on hand. There had to be a tab.

Who was I to argue? This was his territory after all and Godfrey knew how to hold court. I was just a sideshow and knew my place even though it was good to be 'part of the furniture' for once.

'Are you going tonight?' Godfrey suddenly asked and turned to me.

I was momentarily flummoxed. 'Well, yes, of course. Helmut should be good,' I replied flatly.

He raised a glass. 'See you there, it's a decent show and should be fun.'

'A good speaker then?' I prompted a stranger in our midst. Lucky for me, he spoke good English dialect.

'Judging by the first talks, yes, but his wife Isadora, who is a native of Venice and a TV celebrity, stole the show. She will be sadly missed on this occasion.'

'Because of illness?' I asked.

He nodded and finished his drink and headed for the door. Godfrey then departed as well. I followed suit and offered to pay again. A useless gesture by his nonchalant flip of the hand.

'Not necessary,' Godfrey announced.

I knew not to argue and realised that this was one of several visits today for him. I could smell the alcohol on his breath and doubted his initial mention of the art shop in question. Any excuse, eh?

'Will you do the exhibition in London?' I asked nervously.

'Doubtful,' was his stern reply.

"Doubtful" was better than "no".

I smiled to myself.

We then bade farewell and I watched his wide back slowly disappear into the crowd. I wondered how long I would need to stand here before he returned. Everyone had an addiction. I privately laughed at this and headed for the Academia Bridge for my next appointment.

ooo

Helmut was waiting punctually for me, wearing a cream trench coat and a cashmere maroon scarf. With his silver hair elegantly held back by a clasp, he looked a picture of good health. Other than that, he was elderly. Solid German engineering, I noted under my breath.

Then I looked at my unkempt dress code of blue jeans and torn leather jacket and remarked…English crap! I swore to improve my dress sense by this evening…and hoped to bump into a certain woman on my travels.

'Good afternoon,' he announced, 'I like to be early.'

I checked my wristwatch.

'Twenty minutes to be exact,' I announce with pride at my own early arrival, as a group of Japanese tourist jostle us from our vantage point overlooking the boats and gondolas floating by beneath us.

'Excellent,' he observed at my arrival.

I'm impressed by my own time-keeping and made a favourable impression on my latest colleague which made me happy. That is the second time I have achieved this feeling this morning. Must be something in the water. Normally I am shot down by Lillian or one of my customers or an aspiring British artist who is too big for their own boots. Plenty of those but that is a different story to tell. I'll leave that to my memoirs but somehow I don't think I'll be commissioned by a Publisher. There will be scant demand for my observations!

'Where next?' I ask, spinning around in excitement of a new adventure.

'We can just walk,' he says and I follow obediently. We pass down back alleys of food shops, art galleries, lamp shops, and antique establishments…some of which we visit and exchange views on what we have found. We don't have a lot in common at this stage. I am just a visitor, a non-entity. He turns to me.

'Sonia tells me you went to the Guggenheim?' he asks.

'I did, and met her accidentally at reception.'

'Shall we go now and visit the museum?' Helmut asked.

'No,' I say far too quickly.

'Oh, I am not so pretty as Sonia…'

'I didn't expect her to be there and just popped in. She was the added bonus as I don't normally enjoy the exhibits…is it your cup of tea?'

'My what? Oh, I see…I used to live in England and I naturally remember most of the twist on words or odd sayings. No, it is not my cup of tea, as you like to say. I have only been to the Guggenheim twice over the years. I am still baffled by your use of the word "bonus".'

'Wrong use of description, sorry.' I'm embarrassed and now intrigued. 'Where did you live in England?' I quickly asked as a bad follow on in the conversation.

'Lincolnshire.'

'Really. So did my father's dad…'

'I left in 1938 and returned to join up with the German army in Munich before internment took place in England.'

'Whereabouts in Lincolnshire?'

'The Fens.'

'Where in the Fens exactly?'

'Near Wisbech.'

'Wisbech?' This shocked me.

'Yes, why?'

I was flabbergasted still further. We stood in the middle of an antique shop, surrounded by knick-knacks and other assorted rubbish on offer. 'My father's father—my grandfather—was born and lived his whole life in Wisbech.'

'Apart from his war days, of course.'

'Yeah, he joined the army and served in the 1939-45 war.'

'Same as me, although I left the farm in England where I worked the year before and returned to my country to help the cause.' He laughed. 'I was naive back then. Young and eager and somewhat blind.'

'Were you ever a member of the Nazi party?' I enquired tentatively. We did share a past of sorts, after all. I could therefore, within reason, ask him anything. I was pushing my luck with this sensitive question.

'No.'

I rallied against that to no avail. What was I doing? Being so confrontational, which was my way of causing unnecessary trouble. Zip things, I argued silently to myself.

'I recall a "Snow" as it happens who worked on the farm where I worked,' Helmut said.

'Hmm,' I mumbled. 'I wonder if my grandad still remembers your name?'

'I'm surprised he is still alive—'

I cut in, 'Still alive and he spends his last days in a Care Home if he is the same man.'

'There are not many of us who survived the war and live today.' He was suddenly agitated by this news. I ignored this for now.

'Quite,' I said, and vowed to phone my dad when I got back to the apartment in Venice. I was feeling nostalgic and a little intrigued by this parallel storyline.

I changed the subject, but why I did not know. 'Are you nervous about speaking tonight?'

'No. I've done it a thousand times actually. When you have survived the atrocities of the war, nothing disturbs me now.'

'How many books have you written?

'Including this one…three in the Memoir series. Before that, I wrote fiction successfully. Wished I had stuck to that. With a memoir, people generally want a piece of you. Hence, the talk!'

'And have you always given a talk here?'

'My wife, Isadora, was born in Venice and is a TV celebrity on the mainland so it helps, of course, being married to a famous person.'

'Doors open for you.'

Helmut stared at me with curious eyes. 'Absolutely, we are normally here because of her. There is not a great deal of interest in me in Italy, and I speak here because my publisher and my wife asked me to. Equally, I am mobbed back home and the books sell well and Isadora is—as you say—opening doors in this country. We are lucky people. We also have a home here as well. You will see for yourself tonight by the high attendance we attract normally. Tonight is a sell-out. We are fortunate, indeed, to have such an audience.'

'Indeed,' I echoed, and left him to go home before the big event and prepare himself, not that he needed it…a smooth operator, I concluded to myself.

Back at my apartment, I phoned home immediately.

'Dad, are you going to the Care Home tonight?' I asked.

'Yes,' he sighed, 'what is happening to your marriage woes? I have had Lillian on earlier, asking the obvious question as to why you are in Venice.'

Gulp! I ignored his last comment, believing that any private conversation should be kept private. Let's face it, what she really meant was how I could afford such a luxury. 'Dad, if Albert is lucid tonight, ask him about a certain Helmut Grohmann who before the war worked maybe on the farm with him.'

'Helmut who…?'

'Grohmann.' I spelled out the word but it didn't really matter, either Albert could remember or not, depending on how his brain was functioning at his advanced age. We continued to talk about other nonsense and football until conversation was exhausted and I avoided the obvious name of my estranged wife but you can guess who we are referring to.

'Just ask him,' I re-emphasised, with a degree of angst in my voice.

'Got it,' he snarled impatiently, and we said the normal things you say when one is a long way from home. Love and all that. Did we mean it? Not really, but we said it anyway out of duty and it was expected of us, the utterings of family love blah, blah, blah. I showered for the third time (a record for me).

Did I like Sonia that much? Or was I a preverbal dreamer strangled by my own perverse thoughts? Read on and find out.

ooo

The talk by Helmut was an entertaining affair in front of a packed house and I was happy to attend, and spotted Godfrey with a different girl on his arm (one of his models, I assume) but my eyes were, to be fair, looking elsewhere.

Where the damn was she?

Helmut was busy with signing copies of his book for those buying it and by the length of the queue there were plenty of takers. A good night's work for all concerned. Isadora was not to be seen and succumbed to her illness and kept away from the festivities but there was at least two thousand people who crammed the large and imposing room for a speech which centred on nineteen forty-five onward in Florence to the doomed retreat by the German army that same year. Of course, Helmut spoke from his point of view which was both spellbinding and gripping to the avid listener. I couldn't care less but bought a book anyway. In fact, I bought all three volumes. Who was I trying to impress?

Then I spotted Jill. Darn. I tried to hide from her. Where there was one, the other was nearby…I tried to run but to no avail as a familiar voice cut through me like a knife to butter.

'Hi, mister wealthy gallery owner,' Jack boomed in my ear.

I turned and ignored his snide remark. He was already in my face. I had no escape.

'Did you enjoy the show?' he asked. Jill was by now beside him like a faithful puppy and dutifully repeated the question in my other ear.

'Indeed,' I said, looking at them both endearingly in the opulent surroundings. How else could I respond in the circumstances? I was generally bored by war talk. I was here for a possible date. Some hope! Then I saw her in the crowd as well and my spirits suddenly lifted.

Sonia looked serene, all dressed in white and she was also heading towards me! I was stunned by her magnet and momentarily captivated by her beauty and poise and so was the crowd too, who by now seemed to fall at her feet but she kept coming in my direction despite shaking every hand that thrust out and wanted her touch her. I wanted more, and her hand was not on my list of priorities. I told you I was a bit of a dreamer. Let's see where it takes me.

'Hi,' I said, 'great talk. How is your mother?' I've scored my first point with this reference, I thought.

'Not my real Mum. The second wife,' she corrected me. 'She has just a head cold and will live,' she remarked rather nastily.

'But enough to keep her away,' I observed.

'She is resting at our home on the Lido and arrived today, rather than recuperating back in Germany. Just a sensible precaution.' She was guarded at this stage and I admired her sensibility. 'I'm standing in for her…'

'And a fine job you are doing too,' I said, first waving generally at the crowd who gathered around us and then triumphantly holding up the three books for her to see. Jack and Jill stood speechless (was this a first?). I could tell I had impressed Sonia. Another point at our game of, shall I say, tennis, eh? I thought so, to make it easy for you to follow, and tried to impose an advantage.

'Can I buy you a drink after, I know a little wine bar around the corner?' I was wishfully praying for a free drink if they recalled seeing me from this morning's visit. We can live in hope.

'Oh, you mean Cantine Del Vino.' She smiled radiantly. 'One of my favourite places…yes, that would be lovely.'

'So, you have been before?'

'Many times, actually.'

'Me as well,' Jack said. 'Shall we make it a foursome?'

I didn't need this latest intrusion.

I caught sight of Godfrey and cursed silently to myself. He ignored my bedraggled expression and raised a glass of champagne in my direction and then kissed his companion on her left cheek. I was an outsider. I could win this battle but he would somehow win the war, I felt he was telling me. There was something unsavoury hidden here for me to uncover. I only had one day left and he had an entitled lifetime. I would see what could be done, but I was no sleuth. Anyway, it was none of my business. Miracles, however, do happen. I admired the man for his talent but disliked him personally in equal measure.

But why? He was so sure of himself, which somehow grated on me.

Fortunately, Helmut joined us and interrupted the need to answer Jack who suddenly moved away. Jill followed him much to my amusement. I apparently have been let off the hook. But who knows?

'Just these books to sign,' Helmut announced, pointing to a neat pile behind a desk. Then he pointed to me. 'Can we finish our talk tomorrow?'

I didn't know what to say and blurted out something inaudible, followed by a nod of sorts. He jumped on this.

'What time is your flight?' he asked.

'The following morning at ten,' I said.

He beamed. 'Excellent,' he said. 'So we have all day tomorrow unless you have plans already?'

I looked at his daughter and got no obvious come-on. 'I can do my photography early, so basically I can be free,' I announced, and settled for a day of uncertainty in Venice although I was intrigued by him and his family and his apparent connection with Albert.

Then he floored me with his next comment.

'You can fill me in with details of Albert,' he said.

Albert? I never mentioned his name. Where did he get that from? I was by now more than intrigued. I was hooked.

'Where should we meet?' I enquired matter-of-factly.

'At eleven inside St Mark's Square, We'll find each other at one of the cafes,' Helmut said, and then he was gone to sign more of his books for his adoring fans.

Chapter Four

We managed one drink on our own at the Cantine Del Vino, a Bellini for Sonia and I had the red house wine on offer. I couldn't take my eyes off her and it showed but Helmut's comment on naming Albert kept reverberating in my head. That confused me.

'What are you staring at?' she asked, taking a sip of her drink.

'You,' I said, rather confusedly. I was not feeling particularly confident with this comment though.

'I'm flattered.'

I was feeling dangerous playing away on foreign turf. Anyway, point three to me I reckon. Go for it, I urged myself on. I was on match point, according to me!

'You should be,' I remarked casually. 'I've been wanting to tell you since we first met. You are lovely.'

'Flattery will get you everywhere,' Sonia said, with a broad smile.

I gulped at my drink. Where was this leading?

'Do you like being complimented on?' I asked, somewhat bemused.

'Depends on who is complimenting me,' she said teasingly.

'How about…me then?'

'Then I approve. Is this what this drink is all about?'

'It might be…I was rather hoping for your intervention tomorrow but—'

'But my father comes first,' she broke in quickly.

'Indeed,' I said, and leaned over and kissed her. Her open lips were moist and inviting. She was beautiful and I was falling in love with her on this night.

You did that in Venice, right? And I had an empty apartment as well. I felt blessed on this occasion, my legs giddy with excitement. Then Jack and Jill barged in and spoiled everything.

I bought them a drink, it was the right thing to do. The only thing as it happens. We sat at an empty table and shared a bottle of local Vino and then another. It promised to be a long night and I noticed Jack did most of the drinking.

In fact, he was drunk. And boorish. And liked the sound of his own voice. Twice he shot Jill down in flames when she tried to finish his long drawn out stories. I rather liked her punch lines but there you go…you can't please everyone! Her answers were much shorter. Then he kept asking stupid questions of me which I didn't think appropriate. He bored me. What a jerk.

But he was a good artist. Trouble was, he knew it and bragged about it whenever he could. I patiently waited for my turn to speak (or interrupt!).

'Where are you staying?' I asked Jack out of duty. I was dreading his response.

'With a friend near Rialto but the flat is too small to paint in, I have discovered.'

Hence the use of my domain. I wasn't offering though his eyes lit up at the prospect of this invitation.

'When are you leaving, man?' he said pleadingly.

'Monday morning.'

'A pity then,' Sonia said and turned to me. 'I need to go now, and Monday is my last day before returning to Rome. You can always rearrange your flight by one day.'

'Yes, I could,' I interjected among raised eyebrows. And then I pleaded: 'Do you have to go now?' Damn, I had better ideas for the rest of night. Suddenly, Jill's bottom became more appealing. Pity, as I hated the thought of Jack returning to my place which was taboo in my book. They were an item, anyway. Jack seemed to spoil all my fun (or erotic imagination) with his attendance.

Sonia interrupted my dark deeds. 'I'm going back with daddy on his speedboat tonight to the Lido and I have a session with Godfrey booked in the morning at his studio. Besides, you are seeing daddy most of the day tomorrow. I suggest an early night…he can be very challenging but the next day I am free, as you know.'

I didn't need further prompting and vowed to change my flight. I was on match point and didn't wish to involve myself in unfinished business. I wanted a conclusion of sorts. We left our company with them drinking another bottle of local brew, paid up our share of the bill (nothing is free apparently), and I escorted her back to the University near the water front. I knew she was being honest with me because Helmut was waiting for her beside the sleek boat tied up in anticipation for them, before departing across the lagoon. Her goodnight kiss with me was alluring, however, and suggested better days ahead.

I watched them speed off with a wave of my right arm which seemed to down my last energy. I was tired from the day and night. Then I returned to a darkened apartment by way of a slow walk alone, and rang my dad at a crazy hour. I wanted answers before the meeting tomorrow which, as Sonia had explained, was to be rather a challenging one. Helmut had some explaining to do and I wanted to be prepared as best I could.

'What time do you call this?' was my ungrateful greeting. I sighed and suddenly became aware of the time in England.

'Sorry to ring so late, but how is Albert?' I then asked.

'In the circumstances, not bad. Why the concern?'

'Did he remember a German before the Second World War?'

'Sure did. He was in good form actually.'

'Well?'

'Well, what?' he asked with an exhausted tone to his voice.

It was gone midnight back home. I was ringing far too late but I knew he had a phone by his bed. His wife (my mum) had died earlier last year from cancer so I knew I wouldn't disturb anyone. Just my dad actually. Well, he was bleary-eyed by the sound of his voice but it didn't seem to bother me. Perhaps Sonia's odd behaviour (this was in my view) was more than I could bare and someone had to pay. Dad just happened to be in the way of my frustration so he took the brunt of my conversation or lack of it! It suddenly hit me: I was lonely tonight. I prodded him.

'I was hoping for information. I'm seeing Helmut tomorrow.'

'The very German?' he demanded.

'Yes,' I replied.

'Well, Albert remembered him alright. Said if you were to drown him in the nearest canal, he would die a happy man tomorrow.'

'That signifies a good friendship then,' I joked. 'Grandfather actually said that?' I was rather shocked by this.

'Yep, that's what he said.'

'What else did he say, if he still remembered?'

'Plenty.' There was a chuckle in his throat. 'Said that Helmut wasn't to be trusted. That he had hunted him down during the war and intervening years and thought Helmut had perhaps died. He had no idea he was a best-selling author. Is this really the same person we are talking about?'

'Well, yes, he recalls Albert but I will find out more. He even remembered his name which I find strange. Why did Albert want him dead?'

'Because according to him, he was a real bastard…'

I was even more shocked. 'Err, not a reason,' I snapped. 'We need to know why he was considered a bastard in the first place.'

'I'll ask when I next visit. Can I go now?'

'If he still recalls events,' I jibed. But I wasn't showing my smile and dreaded my father's response to my bad humour. If there was any, of course, at this unearthly hour. I put my foot in it again. Dad suffered dementia as well. My future looked almost bright! I am attempting a little black humour here, again! I almost weep at this bleak scenario that awaited me.

He did respond but not as I imagined with his words. I got away with murder.

'Apparently, Helmut saved his life at the back end of the war as they made a pact together of some kind to survive…hardly makes Helmut a bastard, don't you agree?'

'Something bad must have happened,' I remarked. This needed looking into further. I gulped and wished I hadn't called home. It seemed even more weirder as the hours of the forthcoming day passed by quickly for me. I'll come to that.

ooo

I turned off the phone to home and googled the history of Helmut Grohmann and rediscovered his illustrious army career and personal life. He joined the German army in 1938 and then fought in Poland at first, gaining his spurs before serving Hitler all over Europe and the Middle East before the long defeated march back home to Munich after Hitler's suicide and the loss of the war in 1945. He later helped rebuild German cities and entered politics but was unpopular with his ideas over all of Europe and even Germany itself. He later turned to writing to supplement his income and his first thriller, 'To Skin a Cat', became an instant success in his homeland.

There followed two further successful novels and then came his celebrated memoirs which were also a huge hit in his home country and, later, beyond.

In England he spent his teenage years in Lincolnshire where his father was based at Peterborough and worked on tractors. Helmut, later on his return to Munich, first married Claudia, then married his second wife, Isadora Campion, who was making a name for herself on Italian TV. Today, they had homes in Munich, New York and Venice, where her personality first began to flourish.

They raised one child, Sonia, who was born to his first wife who had tragically died giving birth to her late in life. Helmut was by now a worldwide best-selling author and Isadora a national figure on TV. They had no children. She was credited with his success all over Italy. There was more, but I skipped over this. I wanted to know what Albert thought of the teenage years and how he saw things if in fact they were connected as workmen and comrades. So far, they seemed to have different viewpoints of this period in time.

I went to bed eventually both excited and worried, and didn't know why. I checked the time and turned off the light. I tried to think of Sonia naked but my thoughts were elsewhere (damn) much to my irritation staying in this bejewelled city of heavenly dreams alone by myself.

Next morning, rising early I washed and dressed quickly and reread my computer emails and changed flights after securing the house for another day.

I didn't want to miss out on seeing Sonia. Would you do that, being in such a commanding lead? I also got a 'come on' from her. Watch this space.

As it was still early, I photographed local landmarks as the shadows were strong on my lengthy jaunt. I got usable images for my forthcoming Exhibition, which I could adapt weather wise to paint. It was a skill of mine. I, therefore, could do rain or snow or sun so I just needed the set-up basically. If the season was not right, I could alter this as well. These were a last resort, I should add.

Sometimes, the scene under review was perfect to paint. But not often.

I got to St Mark's Square at the allotted time. Fog suddenly descended, shrouding the surroundings in a kind of menace. It reminded me of the work of the modern artist, Pam Masco, who specialised in this type of atmosphere.

Her depiction of Venice was brilliant: ghostly and spellbinding. Helmut called me from a coffee shop on my third circumference without spotting him. I missed him also because of the crowds gathering to see the carnival figures emerging from the shadows and the fact he was partially hidden under an arch. I followed his bellowing voice on my right side.

'Espresso?' he shouted impatiently. A waiter by his side was twitching.

'Latte,' I said to the nervous waiter and sat down next to my illustrious guest.

We had been in a similar situation yesterday: the guided tour. Where was this going to lead? Another lesson no doubt on Venetian culture. Not my cup of tea, if I'm honest with you. I had seen or heard it all before on trips gone by.

Therefore, I will not bore you either.

I waited patiently for my hot beverage.

'I never tire of this view,' Helmut said, with a swish of his left disfigured arm while he drank his coffee using his other hand. 'When you can see it, that is! We are lucky to have a home here.'

'You live on the Lido?' I enquired.

'We do, over 12 years now. We have found our dream house after moving from the Academia area and I want to retire there, God willing. So does my wife who shares my enthusiasm as well because it is very quiet over there.'

'Even with the crowds in the summer?' I said.

'We have walls,' he said.

'Is that enough for your privacy?'

'They are thick and high walls…' he bellowed with laughter. 'then there are the alarms, two dogs…and a gun. Enough, I think.'

We walked the back alleys and narrow waterways and crossed several bridges and popped into every bookshop and spoke to any owners who were suddenly available and I watched Helmut chat to adoring fans who listened to his stories intently. Me? I just stood and stared and wondered why I was a witness to such greatness on my doorstep. I was invisible to anyone on our travels.

He suddenly turned in my direction when we were alone.

'Allow me to be blunt,' he said. 'Last night I saw you kiss my daughter. This must stop.'

'Why?'

'Because I don't want her getting hurt.'

'Do you think I am going to hurt her?'

'Yes. I have my reasons, although these might be unfounded. All will be revealed in time.'

Talk about an over-protective dad. I was stunned by this demand. I said nothing in reply.

On our further travels, he suddenly broke the awkward silence between us and said, 'So, how is Sheila?'

Grandfather Albert's wife died ten years ago and the mention of her name knocked me for a six as well for the second time. We had not mentioned her name either.

'She died from cancer,' I volunteered, 'aged about eighty-eight, I guess. How did you know her?' I quizzed him. 'And you weirdly mentioned Albert and I didn't say his name to you.'

'Sheila and Albert and I were a team on the farm,' he said by way of explanation but I was confused by this. Didn't I just therefore announce the death of someone important to him?

Helmut suddenly dropped his head. Not literally, I should add.

'You all worked together closely until the war,' I said matter-of-factly.

'Yes, until the war,' he replied coldly, without a flicker of remorse knowing I had just announced a death in his so-called adopted family…what had he called it…a team? Sounds the same thing in my world but perhaps I was wrong as I was wrong on most things in life.

'You don't seem upset by this news?' I enquired.

'Actually, I am devastated!' He replied solemnly.

'Didn't you keep in touch after the war?' I asked.

'Obviously not, as we are of a different race and we had countries to rebuild,' he gulped, and raised his eyebrows and then seemed to read my mind. 'I am sorry for your loss,' he added quietly. 'Sheila was a…how do you say it? A great lass, and sadly missed today by me.'

'Now a dead lass,' I whispered to myself. Luckily, he didn't hear my added words and I instantly regretted such a crass description. What was I thinking expressing such bitterness? I made amends by changing the subject and hoped that would suffice.

'Helmut,' I said, 'what were you doing in England anyway?'

'You haven't read my first book,' he said sharply.

I was clearly stumped. It only recorded his version. I had read the first book, but tried to cut corners to somehow satisfy him. 'I'm doing that now but you can enlighten me as I read through it. This period in your life is largely skipped over.'

'My father worked at Benjamin's the tractor engine-maker's as a rep across Europe and we were based near Peterborough. I largely grew up in Lincolnshire and over two years met Albert and Sheila who taught me everything on the farm where we worked every weekend and holidays. In fact, there was so much to do we also worked weekdays as well. It was an idyllic existence.'

'Was Sheila idyllic?' I said pointedly.

Why did I say these things? Then I remembered Sonia's words and I realised this meeting was as challenging as she had warned—more than I feared actually!

'Sheila? She belonged to Albert and they planned to marry…I always assumed they did but as I said, we lost touch regrettably,' Helmut remarked.

'As you said, during the war.' I concluded smartly, wanting to withdraw my comment immediately as my dad's withering words struck home. Why did I always have something to regret? Would I regret putting my flight back a day?

I bought him lunch at one of his favourite Venetian restaurant nearby in the working quarter of Cannaregio district. We ate giant prawns with salad followed by pear tart and cream and a local carafe of white wine and I was happy to pay and return the compliment of his meal at the Hotel Gritti which must have cost a bomb. (Forgive the pun, with reference to the war!) He could afford it! This was my treat and cheap as well. I could afford it!

'Why didn't you resume friendship after the hostilities?' I asked in a reasonable tone.

He just shrugged his shoulders.

This response was not convincing for me.

We hid our differences and talked on a subject close to our heart…banal football chat over coffee.

Tomorrow I would entertain his daughter and would need a bank loan but tomorrow was another day…was she ready for my attention and my devious plans? I couldn't wait to find out. And I was warned off kissing his daughter by Helmut himself! This put a damper on things. For now, I had her staid but strange old father for the day. I smiled nonchalantly and poured more coffee. He was proving far from boring and I couldn't wait to read his history and learn more about, in my mind, his elusive first love, Sheila. My quirky thoughts were obviously on overdrive. Was I right?

Quick as a flash, the sun burst through the lingering fog, bathing the streets with light. It was a magical moment. We walked on after lunch and he introduced me to his terrain of art exhibitions and a Museum of local artefacts, then Casanova's home, and the fish market at Rialto which was by now cleaned down but you could still smell the thousands of years of display and produce selling to local people. It was intoxicating being here at any time.

Several merchants' still remained on the quayside and chatted as Gondolas drifted past on the swollen waters in February. I checked the array of vegetables nearby while my esteemed companion bought a selection of pastries possibly for home from a nearby shop which specialised in cakes. They looked delicious.

'By the way, how is your wife?' I asked rather late in the day, to be truthful with you.

'Not bad, just a head cold. She will live.'

I wished I hadn't asked! I had heard this before. 'Is she here in Venice?'

'She arrived yesterday under a doctor's orders.'

'Are the cakes for her?' I said by way of consideration in the matter.

'Us,' he snapped.

I dropped the subject entirely. Would you persevere with this line of enquiry? I was at my wit's end, which is unusual for me, but I knew I now had to keep my mouth shut.

Chapter Five

This was awkward, and I didn't know in which direction our conversation was taking us to. So I stopped talking, as I explained. Rather I stopped asking stupid questions which I was prone to do at difficult moments on our walk.

There was so much I wanted to know, but fearful of asking in case I intruded on subjects best kept secret. Keeping quiet was not my style, but sometimes silence was the best option, I had learned to my cost.

On the one hand I felt elated and I had achieved my goal of securing next year's exhibitions (except Godfrey) but on the other hand, I was being divorced again this time by Lillian and had fallen into the delightful trap set by Sonia.

How far could we go? Not that she seemed to have an agenda: apart from playing with me and my emotions at a delicate time. It was all of my own making, this stupid game…I just knew how to behave with women (don't laugh at me!) and knew how to please them even if I was the proverbial idiot in the equation and ruined any long standing relationship as a result. (Okay, you have my permission to laugh, not that you need any permission. Just keep the noise down is all I ask of you!) When would I learn from my mistakes?

Why was I never faithful to one person from the beginning? (You are getting louder!) It was like I was always testing or doubting myself. My grandparents were married for fifty odd years and I was impressed by this as well as being impressed by their other achievements in life, until Sheila's untimely death ten years ago. My own father lived on somehow but I was grateful for that despite early signs of dementia and the loss recently of his own wife. Now my health was catching up with me and I didn't like what I was hearing or seeing.

But at least my birth right was set firmly in stone and I gained a certain comfort from this. Or so I believed.

I analysed my personal life. First, there were my marriages to Avril and Carolyn, then Lillian. Each a lovely woman. Then they met me, sadly. It was all downhill from then on. Unfortunately, I was the common factor. I'm left with sad memories to keep me company at night. Oh dear, we have to pay for our sins in the end. What had I done to deserve mine? (Now you are getting even louder with your merriment!)

We strolled the lanes until colliding with the main promenade overlooking The Salute on the horizon. We stood together in St Mark's Square among the winter crowds who were taking photos of the magnificent Doges Palace and elegant surroundings. I was by now transfixed by my companion and didn't want to be an imposition. I checked my watch: a little after four o'clock. I reckon my time was almost over and then I saw him check his watch and knew instinctively our exclusive meeting was up.

'Are you seeing Sonia tonight?' he asked sternly.

'No, tomorrow I assume,' I said slowly.

'What are you doing tonight?' he asked again.

'Well, to be honest, I haven't really thought about it,' I said even more slowly. Really, I hadn't a clue. What would one do in the circumstances?

'Can I meet Isadora?' I suddenly snapped without thinking. I was pushing my luck with this silly demand. In for a penny, in for a pound. Well, that was my reasoning, anyway.

'I don't see why not,' Helmut said, using his mobile. 'I'll just check if it's okay.'

He mumbled something in Italian, smiled, and then turned back in my direction. 'Dinner of spaghetti at six, do you know the Lido?'

'Never been.'

'My boat is waiting nearby. Have tea with us and the boat will bring you back here.'

How could I refuse such an offer? I nodded in agreement. Next minute we were on his luxury speedboat and whipping over the sunlit water. The journey took twenty minutes to the nearby island. We moored up. Then, we walked ten minutes to his walled villa, chatting mainly nonsense about the local terrain. We arrived at the house entrance. The dogs thankfully were not on guard. We strolled the lovely gardens in silence unaware of the female following us a few feet behind.

'Do you like roses?' this person asked and I was somewhat startled by this intrusion. Although it was in Italian dialect, the foreign language was still familiar to me.

I swivelled and was shocked by the woman's appearance. She looked exactly like Sheila at the same age. I had seen old photos. My dad's mum. Albert's wife. Helmut's possible lover. I was now well and truly intoxicated by the unfolding events.

'I love winter roses,' I said by way of a response. I was seeing a double vision and Helmut laughed nervously at my stare and shuffled impatiently on his feet.

This was uncanny, like seeing a ghost. And my staring gave me away. She appeared uncomfortable by my odd behaviour. I was flummoxed by the similarities of the two women. Yes, it was like seeing the past and it momently scared me. I suddenly looked down at the stone crazy-paved path in embarrassment.

'Smell the roses,' Helmut invited me. 'We grow everything here because of the cool climate.'

I did as he instructed.

'Isadora, my darling, I'd like to introduce our guest Martin Snow, an art dealer from London.'

We shook hands rather tentatively on my part, it has to be said. I didn't know what to say and I appeared rather stand-offish. Now I knew where Sonia got her elegance from. And it wasn't from her father.

She took the cake bag from her husband and thanked him with a small grunt of sorts.

'Hello,' I muttered, 'and thank you for inviting me to dinner.'

'Welcome, Martin,' she said. She instantly switched to English. 'Are we eating on the terrace?' she asked, with a broad smile directed to her husband which I had seen countless times before with Sheila in my youth towards Albert.

Isadora now faced her husband and stood very close to him.

'Are you writing tonight, darling?' she asked.

'Probably, after our guest has gone… I'll do an hour before retiring. How are you feeling now?'

She sniffled. 'I am feeling a lot better, I suppose.'

We ate good spaghetti and drank plenty of wine splendidly under a full moon. Isadora drank water. I didn't want to outstay my welcome. It was gone eight and we had exhausted mostly small talk. What can one say further when three appears to be a crowd? Time to go.

'Where are you taking our daughter tomorrow?' Helmut asked and watched intently at me as his wife raised her eyebrows.

'Speak of the devil,' Isadora said, with cute observation.

'Are we meeting tomorrow? I thought you had a flight to catch?' Sonia suddenly said from the direction of the well-appointed kitchen.

I followed her voice. 'I cancelled the flight and rearranged it for the next day.'

'Just because of me?' she asked, seemingly impressed. 'Where are we going?'

Everyone was looking at me as Sonia stepped radiantly out onto the terrace.

I was a beaten man. Helmut's warning earlier still echoed in my brain.

'Wait and see,' I said anxiously. I felt like a rabbit caught in headlights.

'A man of mystery,' Isadora said, with glee in her eye as she cleared our plates away. Sonia sat down at the dining table.

'What time shall we meet?' she asked me.

I was baffled again.

'Oh, I don't know…let's meet at twelve-thirty on Rialto Bridge,' I suggested in the nick of time. I helped clear the table of an assortment of pots and plates to the kitchen and followed my female host. I volunteered to Isadora: 'I went to your husband's book launch.'

'I heard it was good. Usually I attend, especially on home turf, but I've got this hideous head cold so I kept away as a precaution. It makes sense, but word is already out that I am in Venice. Hence, the gathering of press outside.'

'I noticed them. When are you back on the TV?' I asked politely.

'Next week, if I'm okay.'

'That's good. Have you ever been to Britain?' I asked.

'On business, yes,' she said.

'I'm sorry I stared earlier, when we first met.'

She mocked me, 'I'm used to it!'

'Forgive me, but you look like my deceased grandmother when she was younger. The resemblance is uncanny,' I observed.

She smiled politely through me. This was rather odd.

'A bit ghoulish,' she commented.

'Indeed,' I said, and took the coffee and cake out onto the terrace where our host and the daughter waited patiently. Isadora followed with the cream and sugar as I poured the beverage after taking instructions from her. Helmut came first. We sipped and ate in silence but I could tell Sonia was happy to be home. She positively purred.

'Well, thank you for your hospitality,' I said. 'See you tomorrow at our prearranged time and place.' I stood up and moved away from the table and towards the garden. I was very formal in my speech, hiding my nerves.

'It sounds excellent. Are we eating?' Sonia yelled at me.

'We are, straight away, if that is alright,' I replied without a second thought.

What was I thinking? The expense worried me. She was going to be high-maintenance coming from this family. Gulp!

'Sounds fun,' Isadora said, clapping her hands gleefully. 'Can I come?' she suggested, with a flirty question, but unwisely as the head cold still clung on defiantly.

'Mum!' Sonia screamed in obvious mock shock and horror.

This was endearing, considering Isadora was not her biological mother.

However, I could handle one of them, not both. It was a recipe for death. But what away to go, I happily reasoned! I was more than content with this prognosis. The red wine at dinner did the trick for me as my dirty thoughts magnified. Isadora was stunning, if not scary, I had to admit. Helmut was surely a very lucky man.

'I'll ring ahead for the boat to take you back,' said Helmut, picking up his mobile. I felt in a good place but it was time to say my farewells. I kissed Isadora on both cheeks and bade 'goodnight' to Helmut with a firm handshake.

Sonia said, 'I'll walk you back to the harbour front.'

I wasn't going to refuse her offer. We walked slowly hand in hand, surprisingly. The Press sniffed around us for gossip of any kind, but they stayed a few paces behind us.

'Do you miss your real mother?' I gently enquired.

'Of course, I think of her every day.'

'Was she beautiful?'

'From mostly photos, but yes.'

When we got to the boat, I kissed her passionately and she responded. This was illicit according to Helmut, but this also dared me to do this on my current adventure. I was thrilled by this and hugged her and felt her body warmth for the first time. Fuck the accompanying press, who took photographs of us in a clinch for printing in tomorrow's tabloids. We kissed again on the lips before we departed. I couldn't wait for tomorrow and the date, but now I wanted to get back to the apartment and check out things to satisfy my curiosity via phone and computer or reading.

The boat ride was smooth, the spray jetting up behind us. I felt like a king and walked home with a confident stride. I saw Jack but he seemed preoccupied with other things and failed to acknowledge my presence in his furtive mood.

Odd, I surmised. There was no Jill. He seemed in a hurry. Where was he going alone?

I got back and in a mad rush managed to confirm a table for two at the Trattoria Madonna near Rialto Bridge for the next day. I was relieved when they took my reservation and it helped me settle down with Helmut's books and my laptop and a glass of red wine for company. Sprawled out on one of the white sofas, I craved solitude in Venice of all places. It was heaven without conversation and heaven without Jack and Jill for company. I locked the front door and vowed not to answer it if anyone knocked it or rang the bell. I was alone and that's how it was going to stay this evening. Very sad!

According to Helmut's memoirs, he lived in The Fens of England until the outbreak of the Second World War, after Hitler came to prominence in and around nineteen thirty-two and was supported avidly by Helmut's father and later by Helmut himself. He knew my grandfather, Albert, and worked with him at mainly weekends on a farm. It stands to reason he also fraternised with Sheila, who married Albert quickly and went on to have my father, Alec, because she was pregnant with him at the time. Strangely, no mention of this in Helmut's written recollections. Why would he mention this, anyway? I devoured many pages from the first book and then rang my dad.

'Hi, sorry to ring so late but I knew you would be up. Have you seen Albert tonight?' I asked.

'You know I have. I see him every night.'

'How is he?'

There was a moment of silence. 'Not well, since when did you last concern yourself with his health especially being so far away?'

How could I argue with that? He had a point.

'Well, just being polite,' I said.

'Ask him yourself, when time permits,' Alec spat. 'He hasn't got long to live, according to his doctor. I don't think so either. He is ninety-eight after all, and I don't believe he will celebrate his next birthday.'

'That's soon,' I muttered.

'Exactly…'

'I'll be back within a couple of days and will see him then, don't forget to mention Helmut again, an old friend of his before the outbreak of war,' I said.

'He muttered to me that the man needs to get his facts right…'

'How so?' I asked.

'Well, you know how he rambles on…always vindictive when he wants to be and the mention of that name seems to bring out the worst in him. You'll find out soon enough.'

'I will, and goodnight,' I said. There was more to this story and I wanted to get to the bottom of it before my grandfather passed away…and he would, sooner rather than later. Time was against us. I returned to the books and read on feverishly.

I was on a mission this night and, gulp, beyond.

ooo

The next day was bright and cheerful just like my brain. Kidding about my brain! I was actually frazzled from too much reading. Therefore, I woke late and went for a swift walk to help clear my head, showered quickly and took the back alleys to Rialto Bridge for eleven-thirty, one hour before our date. I checked our reservation at Madonna's and booked a gondola for three o'clock. Ever the smooth guy…I was determined to impress her and felt all was appropriate for the afternoon. The evening could take care of itself, such was my wayward confidence. The best laid plans…

Sure enough, one hour later, I met Sonia on the bridge. She looked stunning and I told her so with a kiss on the mouth. She tasted good and I hoped I did too. I wore my only Armani suit (from work), a sharp open-necked shirt and brown Churchill shoes. Although they were work clothes I had travelled in, I felt cool and hoped she had noticed my slick attire. I had certainly admired her: black stockings, Christian Louboutin shoes and a pale blue dress under a cashmere cardigan. Her hair was up and the look of Audrey Hepburn came to mind. Sonia had found a style which suited her. Her make-up was impeccable as well.

'You look good too,' she announced after my compliment to her.

'Thank you,' I responded gleefully. 'Shall we eat? I have a table booked at twelve forty-five.'

'Where are we going?' she asked.

'Trattoria Madonna,' I said, leading her down the steps to the entrance of the restaurant situated in an enclosed alleyway.

'Good choice,' I heard her remark.

'Have you been before?' I asked.

'Several times…it has never disappointed.'

Oh dear, there was always a first time for everything.

I didn't need to worry on that score…we ate like king and queen on lobster with giant prawns and mussels cooked in pasta, followed by apple ice cream and fresh strawberries from the market that day…it was a delicious meal with a delicious woman. The restaurant was very busy, mainly with American tourists.

We finished our Muscadet wine and had coffee. The staff knew her. I felt a little disadvantaged, if I am being honest with you. A swarm of sorts can seem a bit intimidating to me. Especially when I felt out of my depth, despite my cool demeanour. I was a good actor in the circumstances. I had to be.

Chapter Six

I paid the bill in cash. I didn't want Lillian questioning me over this trip and I wasn't giving her any ammunition to use against me when I got home and she peered at an expensive receipt for two at a posh establishment.

This was an innocent meal… even if I had my own carnal motives for later. Sod the words of Helmut. I lived in hope of the relationship between Sonia and I developing. Snigger all you like. I was on a roll.

'When are you coming to London?' I asked.

She lowered her eyes lids. 'Maybe sooner than you think. It depends…'

'On what?'

'I have to tread carefully. Remember, I am still married and going through a divorce.' she said sadly.

'Ditto,' I said.

'It's all a bit soon. Tell me about your wife.'

I was baffled. This was not how the conversation was supposed to go, having touched on this subject fleetingly at the Guggenheim Museum earlier.

We drank more coffee at a café this time. I ignored her then, but I gave myself away fully this time (unusual for a man) and weakened my cause. Which was what? I hear you ask. Good question. Why did I choose therefore to weaken my cause? Beats me, but I obviously wanted to unburden myself. The pressure valve needed to be released. I chose to relieve myself with verbal diarrhoea. I told her everything about my life. She was a good listener, thankfully.

'What's wrong?' Sonia asked finally, with confusion in her voice.

'Your dad has warned me not to kiss you,' I muttered sheepishly eventually.

'Well, you haven't stuck to that rule,' she said. 'That is his over-protective nature, warning many men off me, you included.'

'Many?'

'Several, over this past year as they heard of my marriage collapse. I am desirable in the great scheme of things, I should add!'

That brought nervous laughter from the both of us.

We took our gondola ride, which seemed to surprise her and delight her in equal measure. Cringeworthy, but it was the obvious thing to do in Venice.

Expensive but worthwhile and romantic. We sat back in comfort and let the oarsman take us on a watery journey for the next forty-five minutes while I continued my tale of woe.

'Lillian, my current wife, is her name,' I explained awkwardly. 'She will be forty next birthday. I first met her in London and yes, before you ask, we have been to Venice before.' I was supposed to be dodging the questions and I felt weird being so closely interrogated by Sonia.

'I wasn't going to enquire,' she reassured me, before dropping a little bombshell. 'What does she do professionally?'

'Ugh!' I groaned at this comment, before adding, 'Lillian is a solicitor specialising in marital law, if you must know!'

'Specialising in what…?' She asked again incredulously.

'Yep, divorce. You couldn't make it up!' I laughed again. But this time it was a more nervous reaction.

'Ouch!' She screamed in part shock and part mocking joy.

'You could say that,' I said. 'How long have you been together or apart from your husband?' I asked wearily.

It was twenty questions time. I felt exhausted by our sword fighting.

'Four years, I guess,' she answered. 'That is, we have been apart that long.' Then she said pointedly, 'Is there a chance of a reconciliation with Lillian?'

'No,' I replied sharply. Phew.

'How many times have you been married, did you say?'

I was on thin ice with this one. 'Three times,' I uttered rather timidly. Time to turn the tables. 'And you?' I asked.

She ignored me. 'What were their names?'

Bloody hell. She was like a dog with a bone. 'My first wife was called Avril and that lasted twelve years approx. and my second wife was called Carolyn and we lived together about the same time.' I sounded like a bloody lothario.

'Oh, a twelve-year itch then rather than the customary seven years…'

'Pardon?' I questioned. 'Oh, I see. I hadn't thought about it like that…perhaps you are right in your assumptions.' It puzzled me, but I went along with her assessment anyway. It made for an easier life.

'Just surmising,' she said, with a thin smile (or was it a grimace?).

'Just surmising?' I responded. 'Are we having our first tiff?' My giggle was rather forced. I was just beginning to feel better about myself. Not the lousy bastard I was painted to be by those women I married back in England. I still possessed some redeeming features if Sonia at the very least fancied me. I let my mind wander. It was the best solution, for me at any rate. Or so I thought.

'No, we are not having a tiff!' She said gleefully.

I was let off the hook at this precise moment. My heartbeat went back to normal.

'By that reckoning, I have about twelve years with you. I am now forty-nine-ish so I will be sixty-one approximately when you dump me,' I calculated.

Sonia pulled a comical face. 'Hmm, I will have to consider it. Could be fun. Have you ever been violent or a bully to any of your wives?' she asked.

'Never and never.'

'That is something in your favour,' she said. 'Sounds tempting.'

Our gondola came to the end of its journey and I paid again using cash. Apart from the inquisition, it was an interesting day and I had fallen big time for the woman holding my arm.

'And you?' I asked, with a certain devilment in my voice that hovered between us.

'What are you suggesting?' Sonia responded mischievously. She knew exactly what I meant.

We strolled the back alleys and I pointed out where Whistler once stood to paint the view in front of him. We stopped for coffee and cake in a café.

'Well?' I persisted.

'Before Peter?' she asked playfully.

'Who is Peter?' I asked.

'My soon to be ex-husband. Once before, I married foolishly in my twenties, before I had an affair with Peter. So it will be twice when I get divorced again.'

I asked the usual questions and then went for the jugular, 'Have you ever been violent to a man?'

She hesitated, before consuming her little chocolate cake. The cafe was packed with customers and she spoke solemnly and quietly, 'My first husband, Erich, was an alcoholic. unknown to me, and he was abusive when drunk. One day I hit him in retaliation. So yes, you could say that.'

'Not counted,' said I quickly. 'Unlike your father, of course, who was violent to many men in the war.'

'Not counted,' she replied equally quickly. Sonia picked up on my sarcasm by the manner of my speech. 'Violent conduct in the war, that's an entirely different thing. He was just trying to survive and was under orders like all soldiers whoever you fought for. And the opposition were not men but soldiers who wore uniforms so they were legitimate targets,' she said with sadness in her eyes. 'Anyway, it does at least prove you have read most of his memoirs…'

'I have, and so far I have reached a lot of deaths.'

Sonia looked at me sternly. 'Book two, at least. Do you like the style of writing? It was a best-seller.'

'Yes.'

'I was the editor,' she said proudly. 'I edit each book for him.'

'Really? Very slick. So you are aware he was brought up in England?'

'Hardly brought up actually. He lived there for two years between 1936 and 1938, as his father got a job in engineering in your country.'

'On tractors. Helmut knew my grandfather.'

'In Lincolnshire?'

'Yes.'

'Then you must be related to… Albert!' She shrieked.

'I am,' I said quietly. How did she remember this name?

'Is he still alive?' she asked nonchalantly.

'Still alive, now ninety-eight or more… It stands to reason your father knew Sheila? No mention of her in his memoirs.'

'Sheila who?' she asked.

'Sheila O'Dowd. My grandmother.'

'Remember, I was just the editor of the written word.'

I smiled ruefully, 'Helmut has selective memory,' I added.

'So sorry to eliminate Sheila…just not vital, I suppose, to events. I had no idea of her importance.'

'Indeed. One man's version of a story is not shared by another man, I guess.' I stated, with a shrug of the shoulders.

'Hmm, sorry again. You will have to ask him why he left her out.' I was perplexed.

'Or Albert,' I remarked.

'Or Albert, but at least he got a mention,' she echoed, the first part of mutual history in unison with me, adding: 'He spoke of him privately, of course, and that's how I know of him but it seems he and her were largely airbrushed out of his memory…'

I looked at her apprehensively.

'You wouldn't think he had lived those two years,' I said coldly.

We did not make love that night. The *Mansarda* was fine as a house and studio but not conducive to the likes of Sonia, who was used to luxury in this mostly renaissance city. Well, that is my excuse anyway! The warning words of her father hung heavy in the air. He was getting to me. Besides, she had an early flight to catch the next day. The house I occupied had its uses and was not a romantic bolt hole after all. I just wanted to get home and hear Albert's side of the story. Could he be trusted? Was his memory still sharp? Did he recall Helmut well enough so many years down the road? After all, Albert had dementia and was in a Home to see out his dying days in comfort. This investigation, therefore, would be challenging!

Let's rewind a little. I walked Sonia to the boat. We were largely quiet but held on to one another like our life depended on it. Pathetic, really.

'Will you see Albert?' Sonia asked.

'I will,' I said.

'Has daddy not been fair to him?'

'…Well, so far he has not, although eliminating him is better than giving criticism in his memoir,' I observed, giving her a farewell kiss on the lips. The captain of the boat saw us and gave an order to cast off. I was grateful for that, I hated long lingering goodbyes. I wasn't in the mood anyway. Our conversation was becoming a passion-killer.

'Is your dad coming to London?' I asked.

'Not that I know of. Why? Do you need him to?'

I thought about this.

'No,' I added, 'I want to see only you.'

She kissed me ferociously in full view of everyone. I let her play this game and I played mine. We were good at games. Or control. This was going nowhere until I discovered the truth of why there was so many lies in the air.

We all played them to gain the upper hand. Someone would come crashing down, it just wasn't going to be me, in spite of my poor deck of cards. Who held all the aces in the pack?

'Good, that is all I need to hear,' she whispered. 'I'm in London soon. May I ring you?'

'Can't wait,' I said with a wave.

Then she was on the boat as it sped away across a lagoon. I turned and went back to the *Mansarda* on foot. I read Helmut's books until gone midnight, taking notes whenever I needed to, for reference only. Trouble was, there was a lot of notes to unscramble in my mind. I hoped Albert's brain was up to scratch to help unravel those missing years from Helmut's memory. If not, we were buggered. I packed my clothes and emptied the fridge for my departure in the morning.

Chapter Seven

The flight home from San Marco to Gatwick was bumpy and our landing rather bumpier. Luckily, everyone on board survived… ha! ha! A collective clap followed from the passengers. That is what you get with a cheap flight! A bad landing, I should add, in case you thought I was referring to the clapping.

We touched down in the thunderous rain. No one picked me up. The journey home was by taxi. Expensive in the morning. I had breakfast on my own in my apartment: scrambled eggs and black coffee and an offending text from Lillian came through. I read it then ignored it.

The eggs were good though. And the coffee okay. I got back to my office/gallery at noon and checked for any sale of paintings by the staff while I was away. There weren't any sales. My mood worsened and so did the afternoon. The hours ticked by slowly. It remained deathly silent. I stayed on after hours but to no avail. Even in London, there were slack days.

We now had twelve in a row. A disaster.

I regretted the money I spent in Venice, especially on Sonia. But I didn't regret the artists I had booked for mixed shows, including Godfrey's One-man exhibition in May next year. He said 'yes' by text after consulting with his wife.

Some things excited me. This was one. I stayed on the gallery premises until six-thirty but it was useless. I took nothing. I got home at Wapping, had tea of cold chicken and hot chips and warm baked beans (a bit different to lobster pasta) but I had to economise somewhere. I started with the food shopping budget. Then I travelled to see Albert where I hoped the fun would start, or heartache, I wasn't sure what would confront my barrage of queries.

When I saw him, I first said, 'How are you?'

He looked at me quizzically. 'Fair to middling.' I was in for one of those nights, and returned the stare. He was probably going to be bombastic with me. Hold on to your hat, if you are wearing one. It promises to be a rough ride.

'Just got back from your favourite place,' I said, with hope in my voice.

'What…Bognor!' He replied, as quick as a flash.

I was stumped, having never been to any part of the south east coast, much to my shame. I always wanted to visit Brighton. We can live in hope!

'Venice,' I stated in reply. That would cheer him up.

'Never been to the place,' he said matter-of-factly.

Oh, dear.

I sighed. 'Dad told me you have been six times since the war…'

'You can't trust him.'

'Actually, I do trust him,' I said, without any sign of rancour. I knew I was in for the long haul tonight.

We sat in the communal lounge at the home in Carshalton and it was full of old people, I reckon Albert being the oldest inhabitant. I could smell the piss. I was offered a cup of tea by one of the uniformed staff.

'How is he behaving?' I asked her quietly on the side.

'Well, he hasn't upset anyone…yet,' was her dry response. 'Albert is a good resident generally.'

At two thousand pounds a week, that was exactly what I was expecting to hear. Money was fast running out at this rate. If he lived here another year, then the financial onus would fall on me to help, having sold his house in the first place to pay for this environment. I didn't have the funds to support him what with the divorce looming on the horizon. It stood to reason he would die before then because of his advanced age…I was hoping! Yes, I was callous in my viewpoint. But he was defying the odds, I cursed under my breath. I loved him, but I was largely broke, and he living long weighed heavily on my mind, especially as he seemed to like it here.

'Six times, you say?' he said, counting slowly on his bony fingers.

'Which? Bognor or Venice?' The nurse suddenly enquired.

We all laughed at the jokey observation.

'Well, the one with the most canals,' Albert said with a smirk on his face.

'That would be Venice then,' came the familiar male voice from the left. We all looked over to the man interrupting our conversation.

'Dad!' I yelled and went over and hugged him.

'Smart ass,' Albert said. 'Venice it is then. What were you doing there?' he asked me.

'Working mainly. I saw an old friend of yours.'

'Ah, Helmut. The old scrounger. I thought he was dead. Must be as old as me.'

'Yes, about the same,' I guessed.

'A writer?' Albert said.

'A successful author,' I added. 'He has written two best sellers, a successful screenplay and his celebrated Memoirs. His wife works on Italian TV.'

'Ah, his Memoirs. What piffle! My son tells me I am hardly mentioned, and Sheila not at all,' Albert observed with a howl. Was this anger?

'Piffle?' I said.

'All lies.'

'So you have read all three books?' dad said, interrupting us. The nurse had by now moved on to another patient in a similar room down the corridor.

'Don't need to,' Albert said. 'Why should I help line his pocket? The war has been very profitable to him.'

'You don't approve?' I asked cautiously.

'I should have killed him when I had the chance,' Albert stated.

'When did you first meet?' I asked.

Albert looked at me and then dad and back to me. '1936 or thereabouts,' he said.

'And Sheila?' I said.

'Can't answer for the dead. About the same time, I guess.'

'When did he leave England to go home?' dad enquired. He was asking my questions, bless him. I suddenly felt redundant.

'Oh, I don't know. The outbreak of war interrupted us all...I would think towards the middle of 1938. Yes, that would be about right,' Albert replied with a shrug of the shoulders.

'Germany invaded Poland and they recalled everyone home who were living abroad,' dad said. 'Seems an obvious thing to do,' he added.

'Before their internment the following year,' I said.

'Yes, Helmut suddenly was up and away with his family wearing the same clothes on his back,' Albert explained, in a solemn mood.

I was dumbstruck by this remark and my brain went into overdrive.

'According to Helmut's memory, the book states he departed these shores at this time, the year you were born, dad.'

Dad looked at me strangely, as if I wasn't supposed to work this equation out.

'Not a word on leaving this country,' said Albert bitterly. 'Here one minute, gone the next.'

'You sound angry,' I said.

'I was. We did everything together. Could have least told me he was leaving these shores.'

We all pondered this.

'War was looming. Perhaps his parents didn't give him any notice,' dad said.

'Accordingly—' I started but dad interrupted my flow, again. He had obviously read the Memoirs better than I had.

'—in his book,' dad announced, 'he was given just "three hours' notice" to leave. His account, anyway.'

'Rubbish,' said Albert. 'He had all the time in the world. He spoke to Sheila before he left…he had time to do that.'

'Then he was gone,' dad said.

'How old was he in 1938?' I asked.

'Twenty or thereabouts, I reckon. Could have been older. We didn't discuss our ages,' Albert said.

'How old were you?' I asked.

'About the same,' he replied.

I thought about this. That made Helmut nearly ninety-eight as well, but he appeared a lot younger-looking than Albert. In fact, Helmut looked a lot younger. That's what having money and privilege and fame did! And an added scalpel held in the hands of a private surgeon! Just saying!

'How old was mum?' dad asked.

A million questions to answer. Albert was getting tired by this and I saw the nurse with tea hovering in the background, ready to pounce on our incessant grilling of one of her patients. At two thousand pounds a week, he was worth preserving a little while longer at this home, I guessed she was thinking.

'Oh, Sheila was roughly two years younger,' Albert mumbled.

'And then you married?' I said.

'What else was I to do?' Albert suddenly snapped. 'I had a baby on the way and I loved her. That was the right thing to do in those days; I didn't want a bastard child to help bring up.'

'The right thing to do,' dad beamed.

I was ultra-cautious and hugged dad again, fearful of asking any more damaging remarks. The nurse moved in on Albert.

'Time for bed,' she said.

I was ready for mine.

Skipping through the concluding pages of Helmut's last book, I had lots more questions to ask Albert and vowed to see him again…and soon. I wanted to find out about the 'facts', according to his take on things. Time was running out.

Albert was elderly and was one of the last warriors still alive from the Second World War. He didn't attend memorial services, preferring a silent prayer of his own. He was a private person and didn't like publicity. His version of events was worthy of listening to, if he remained clear in his head.

Other than that, like all veterans, he didn't talk about the horrors of what he saw. I was doubtful of his words but time would tell, assuming we had any.

I rang the Care Home in Carshalton after a foggy night's sleep.

'How is Albert in room six?' I enquired from reception.

'Fine. Do you want to speak to him?' came the reply.

'No,' I said, and cut the line dead. Then I rang dad at his workplace, he was a taxi driver in Surrey.

'Are you seeing Albert later?' I asked him.

'Of course; I told you, I see him every day.' came the curt answer.

'Will you see him soon?'

Silence. 'About half an hour, depending on my latest fare and the traffic.' He then asked solemnly: 'Why?'

'Oh, just make sure he is okay and give him my love.'

'A funny thing to say. When shall I tell him you will call over again?'

'Tomorrow, got some reading to do first.'

'Ah, Helmut's Memoirs?' he said.

'That's right,' I stated. 'Got to get my facts right.'

I heard him sigh on the phone. It was that loud.

'Or plenty of lies by the author to consume,' he snorted.

Chapter Eight

How often have you woken up and questioned your lifestyle?

I scrubbed my teeth at the bathroom sink and asked myself the same thing.

Lillian phoned and I ignored her call. She would only antagonise me still further if the future of Bolly came up. Our dog meant everything to me and was in Lillian's care temporarily. She was just using Bolly as a bargaining chip and I wasn't in the mood to fight my corner rationally. Not yet anyway. I had not even answered her text, so I was in big trouble for my non-action. She was aware of the law, damn it. That was her profession. It made things tricky between us.

Now, about my lifestyle. I had been in the art business since my teens and a sole gallery owner since my dad retired from the business and doodled in taxi driving to make ends meet while Albert lived on in the Care Home. Petrol cost was becoming an issue. Someone also had to pay for Albert's room at a Care Home when monies ran low. I paid what I could afford, which was very little and that went straight to my dad for his own upkeep (god forbid!). Soon, depending on my dad's health, I would be responsible for the lot, fair enough.

I wanted to financially help dad. That part was a given.

Lillian knew this. She was caring, but it was a sticking point in our now sour relationship. I was good at my job but frustrated by the lack of money people spent on the high street. It got worse as the years slipped away and I observed a gradual drop of confidence in the public spending sector. What could I do but fight on? I didn't know of an alternative. We were in central London and dealt with all nationalities but this was a global problem, hence the financial predicament. My rent was high and so was my business rates. Turnover was either static or ten percent lower each year and this was the problem. I struggled on but it was a losing battle and that is why I went to Venice in the hope of finding the salvation. Godfrey Snapp promised a new horizon. I lived to fight another day. Well, that was the plan (and hope).

I finished washing my face and dressed formally for work but I was miserable. Sonia can cheer me up when she comes over and contacts me if I'm in the mood for her or my antics desire it! Shallow again, I hear you shout.

What would you do in the circumstances? I too have needs to satisfy. I go to work feeling down and empty of spirit. I could have washed windows for a living, but I don't want to insult anyone's trade. Becoming a window cleaner suddenly appealed. Cash was king. And I needed cash, as I didn't have any sales. And then I thought of Sonia again. She was there for the taking and my way out of this financial mess. I told you I was untrustworthy or callous or both. Make your own mind up at the end of the story. But she was beautiful and would have many admirer's, so speed was of the essence. I was good (or bad) at being callous, depending on your viewpoint.

At work, I tried to conclude a deal before closing but I was perturbed by Helmut and his version of events. But I got the sale, despite my gloom.

Yippee! Back to the problem in hand. Supposing Helmut left England for different reasons other than the declaration of war? I know what you are thinking…and it had crossed my mind as well. So we are all bastards. Let's get this out in the open…you think dad is Helmut's son and not Albert's hence the antagonism simmering in the background. If that was the case, this would make me of German blood. I'll tell you what, I will ask someone in the fucking mix. How about that? The prospect made me shudder, though.

So I did. Just like that. Trouble is, Albert isn't playing as his brain has gone AWOL. Bloody typical, I say.

So I asked dad, man to man, face to face. Thought you might be impressed.

'Are you suggesting that Albert isn't my dad? Have you gone completely mad?' Alec roared. 'I even look like him,' he concluded. It was true, he did look like Albert but then he had never met the German in the flesh. I had, and it was frightening at their similarities. For me anyway.

I had tried ringing Albert earlier at the Care Home again, but he was fast asleep and not, therefore, available to talk to.

My dad's face was ashen with rage. 'I have been visiting him every day or night since Sheila's death. What are you saying? Spit it out, man!'

'That maybe you are okay with it. After all, like you, I love Albert and will do so forever.'

'In spite of him maybe not being my real dad? Get real. This news would change everything we hold dear. Besides, my mother is British, that will not change. My birth certificate says I am English.'

'That can be distortion of the facts to suit the circumstances of the time. At least you were not illegitimate. Science may prove who your dad is though.'

'I know who my dad is. I will always love Albert, despite any science telling me differently.'

I looked at him, with his eyes ablaze with anger and confusion. 'I know, I know,' I retorted. 'Only Sheila knows the truth or we conduct a DNA test,' I said. 'And Sheila won't be talking…' I added quietly.

'A bloody what?' Alec replied indignantly.

'A DNA test.'

'You think that will alter my mind? You have to understand the sacrifice my father made…'

This was his reaction the next day as well. He was looking at the sleeping figure of Albert in his chair. 'This man brought me up single-handedly with Sheila, so they will always be my parents…'

'Precisely,' I said. I looked away and staring into nothingness.

'Precisely?' Echoed Albert, awakening from his slumber. 'We need to know the truth.'

'What?' Alec shouted in a bewildered state.

Albert sat up. 'I suspected they were having an affair. Then suddenly, Sheila got pregnant, Helmut left the country and war broke out. I did the decent thing and married a pregnant woman and thought (he pointed a finger at my dad) you were mine…now, I'm not so sure.'

'Not so sure?' Alec said in a disgusted manner.

'Perhaps Sheila was right all along,' Albert said.

'About what?' I asked.

'What is your middle name, son?' Albert asked, searching the face of the man he thought of as his own. We all knew the answer but it still needed to be voiced.

'Dieter,' Alec said sheepishly.

'There you have it,' said Albert. 'Sheila wanted it as a first name but we thought differently because of the war and the bureaucratic issues at the time. She wanted to state your possible heritage, and this was her way. She didn't know for sure who the father was. But circumstances at the time prevented the use of this name. Alec was a patriotic name in the circumstances. We didn't want trouble on our doorstep, especially as I was away fighting on the continent.'

'And there lies the rub,' I said.

'What does that mean?' Albert replied alarmingly.

'Well, according to his memoirs, Helmut served in Africa, Egypt and most of Europe…'

'So?' Albert said.

'Exactly your route,' I said. 'You followed him everywhere, but your paths never crossed, until you met in Europe.'

'We finished in Italy.'

'The Po Valley…'

'That's right, near Florence,' Albert said. 'The war was over. The retreat started from here.'

'So did your last chance to kill him legitimately,' said I.

'I had my chance. Should have taken it,' Albert said quietly. 'But you have to remember he saved my life. And we had a history, however unsavoury it was.'

ooo

'Why should I doubt who my real father is?' Alec said on the phone to me when I got home.

I had made supper of egg and cheese on a toasted bagel and was eating this when the phone went off. I mumbled my response with my mouth full. 'You shouldn't,' I managed to say.

Dad suddenly interjected, 'But now, after all these years, I am beginning to doubt it. I wish you hadn't gone to Venice and met Helmut accidentally.'

'So do I.'

'Why do you believe him or his books?' he asked.

I thought about this. 'I don't necessarily, but we only have Albert's version of events to counteract this which are unreliable and Sheila is dead. There is only one place to go to find the truth…Helmut has actually said very little, but the implication is there from him, and we have largely been glossed over in his Memoirs.'

'A DNA clinic is your suggestion.'

'Yes,' I said, holding my breath. This was a pivotal moment.

'Okay, I will do it,' said my father without protest.

I was lost for words.

'We need the truth,' he said.

'We all need the truth,' I confessed. Our destiny was perhaps not as straightforward as we thought. The news affected me as well.

Reading the Memoirs again, I was convinced of the truth: that my dad was not Albert's son and therefore Helmut was my grandfather and I had German nationality in me. Why ignore Sheila in the books though? Unless Helmut wanted to hide a secret? That made Sonia and I blood-related: that put a cat among the pigeons! Or were we? Perhaps I was wrong in my assumption.

All we needed was confirmation of the DNA, which would reveal the truth that surrounded Albert and Helmut. One of them was a real father to my dad. If Sheila was alive, she could reveal all without the obtrusive need of asking for tests but sadly she was no longer alive. Who said she would reveal anything, anyway? But my father's middle name disturbed me. It was a tribute to Helmut, surely?

Helmut first moved to England and Lincolnshire as an eighteen-year-old in 1936. His father supported Hitler since this man won an election in 1932 and the state voters soon followed him. There was great unemployment in Germany at this time, and this represented, through disillusionment, a vast vote for him. Hitler knew this and played on this. He couldn't lose an election this way with their massive backing. Under him, the Jewish community was to be expelled. The rest was history.

Helmut worked part-time at weekends on Picket Farm on the Fens and met many local boys and girls. Albert and his girlfriend Sheila were two who were to become his closest friends during his stay. Over the next two years, they became inseparable during the troubles brewing on the horizon. Sadly, Helmut, because of his name, was soon victimised by other less friendly kids and his family suddenly packed their belongings and left to go back to Munich. Locals blamed the war factor problem on their departure to which Helmut hinted at in his books. He mentioned the Purity Act in his recollections but not Sheila and Albert during those formative years. Odd. I wasn't convinced by their omission. Are you? Surely the whole point of a Memoir was to tell it how it happened, warts and all, and assume the reader wants the whole truth and nothing but the truth. You don't just airbrush people out.

I would ask Helmut but it had to be to his face. I could not read his facial expressions on the phone or rely on Skype or similar. It was not my way. I wanted my questions answered quickly. I booked an immediate flight again to Venice from Gatwick. It was tomorrow but that would do. The airline decided availability, not me. I had no time to waste and anyway I felt restless by not having any news. As I paced the gallery floor, I was thirsty for information.

Any.

I phoned the Care Home once more and followed my gut instincts for information. I was on the prowl. Albert apparently didn't have any gut instincts at the moment. These sadly evaded him.

The receptionist said, 'Albert is not necessarily seeing anyone tonight owing to memory loss and he won't be leaving his bedroom. Visitors are restricted to family members only and then for a restrictive timespan.' The woman did not mince words. 'He is tired and we want him to rest without further interrogation.'

So that was that. I got the message loud and clear, even though I was family.

I packed for my trip to Venice and had a beer to cheer me up. Something had to cheer me up. The alcohol did this, or so I convinced myself. My phone rang and on picking it up my dad confessed: 'Although I can see my dad tonight, it is best to let him sleep uninterrupted.'

'Apparently, he has no conversation and he doesn't want to see anyone, anyway,' I added.

'But I'm not just anyone…' He was almost crying.

I was unsympathetic but don't why this is the case. I nearly said he might be, but thought better of such a crass comment and it wouldn't necessarily raise a laugh but privately I found it funny until I thought of my situation. Then I suddenly felt sick. That was the problem for me.

'I am off on my travels, dad. You will have to hold the fort until I return. I am closing the gallery to save on extra costs.'

'Where are you off to?' he asked.

'It's obvious.'

'Venice,' he said. 'Should have guessed.'

'Coming?' I asked.

'Haven't been invited.'

'Only because you wouldn't like the questions being asked.'

He scoffed at this remark and answered: 'And you wouldn't like the answers thrown back at you and Helmut from my direction!'

He was probably right. After all, several days ago, I had never met this German gentleman before and was set in my ways as to who my grandfather was. Now, I was deeply disturbed…I needed answers as to my real lineage.

Seemed like a natural plan to go there, but someone would get hurt along the way. I didn't care, I was like a bulldozer. as long as we got at the truth. After all, was my granddad a victorious Englishman or a vanquished German? At the very least, I wanted to know. Others thought differently. Helmut did and distorted the past to suit his readership. He liked the adulation from his fans (their money was vital) and there was a lot of them to keep pleasing! And so it went on and on. The customer was always right. So give them more of the same…courageous lies! It worked at the beginning. Therefore, stick to a winning formula. The publisher would also be very happy.

Did everyone want the truth? I doubted it as too many people would suffer and we wouldn't want that, would we? A publishing empire would collapse.

What a shame! The past had too many secrets anyway. If I delved still further, I would absolutely open a can of worms. That was my forte. Oh dear, I hear you groan! Best keep away if you have a weak bladder then.

I carried on and said to my dad, 'I have to ask the questions, even if I don't like where it takes us. You are still my father, right?'

'Right!'

'So, when are you having the damn DNA test?' I asked rather too hastily, but at least the ball was rolling.

'As soon as Helmut or Albert does,' he answered.

That silenced me.

Chapter Nine

I was at a crossroads. I returned to Venice. Helmut looked at me. Correction, Helmut looked through me. I felt uncomfortable but this was never going to be easy.

I repeated to him: 'Did you have an affair with Sheila?' My eyes were alert. With…what actually? Was I bitter or baffled or felt cheated?

I asked again.

'Read the book,' came his prolonged response.

'It's all bullshit,' I raged, 'just to please your hordes of readers. Sheila doesn't even get a mention. It is so sanitised as to the early days in England. It makes you a hero. It starts with an enlightened stay in England, perfect for those wanting the perfect memoir but you forgot to mention what really happened.'

'That tells you everything you need to know!' He was critical with his tone. 'What really happened?' He questioned himself aloud.

'That you had an affair with Sheila.'

'Yes, I did fall in love with her, but it was short-lived, so I omitted it.'

'But it was enough to saddle my dad by an odd middle name…'

'Which was?'

'Dieter.'

'That was Sheila's choice. Nothing to do with me.'

We stood on the steps of The Salute. It was a cold day, our words cascading off the wintry wind into each other's stern features as we faced one another close up. We were both wrapped up in heavy knee-length coats. We looked like two soldiers squaring up to each other.

'What is your…. dead brother's name?' I asked.

'Dieter,' he said.

'Hmm, how convenient, it was her way of paying homage to you all,' I said.

'Or coincidence,' he said wryly. Then he announced, 'Sheila married Albert after all.'

'Only because she didn't agree to your ultimatum,' I said smugly.

'What ultimatum? Besides, she would be an English girl living in my country. I wouldn't put her in such a precarious position.' Helmut asked, stepping back and giving us a little space at one of the side entrances of the church. Thankfully, it was quiet on this day, even the peel of bells from the towers seemed dull over the surrounding choppy water. Fortunately, so was our language in spite of our hostility. I stared beyond him for a second. The vista was stunning and the boats on the canals slow and elegant. It was a shame we were at loggerheads on this occasion.

I drank in the idyllic view and cursed my situation. Why did I do this to my family? Hang on, who was my family? Was the man who stood in front of me now called my Grandfather? My birth certificate said I was English. Was this now wrong? I shuddered in the cold at the thought of it. What ultimatum? Helmut had asked. I pondered on this before replying.

'The one you gave her: come back to Germany with me, now. Or words to that affect. She was pregnant. Possibly with your child,' I said, wary of my own voice. Was he scared of my increasing booming voice? It seemed not!

'What proof have you got?' he enquired, sounding like a commander in the army. Direct.

'None. Just a hunch really. Albert doesn't talk about this episode or the war to be honest. Are you up for a DNA test?'

'I'm a married man. What do you think?'

'She doesn't need to know…' I said.

'She is already suspicious,' he announced.

'Of our meeting?' I asked.

'Isadora wanted to come to Venice. How long are you here for?'

'I didn't think she would find our conversation enthralling.' I thought about this. 'Perhaps she would…after all, she is the spitting image of Sheila.'

'Another coincidence, I think,' he remarked with a winning smile.

'That makes two so far, and we've only had this one chat today,' I said triumphantly. 'I seem to be on a roll.'

'You do,' said Helmut. 'Let's have something to eat and see where things take us.'

I was up for that. On both counts.

ooo

'How long am I here for?' I reminded myself to his question, but to no one in particular, but Helmut sat opposite me and obviously heard me as we tucked into a seafood platter at one of the popular restaurants near the Rialto bridge. So I was addressing him with my idle comment. There was plenty of choice of good restaurants in the vicinity but Helmut liked the view of the gondolas passing by the quayside from where we sat at our table. We drank white wine with the mixture of local seafood on our plates…langoustines, prawns, squid, mussels, the food and drink was truly wonderful, it had to be said. It beat the usual cheese and pickle bap from Greggs back in London.

. 'As long as it takes actually,' I added and stared at him.

'And how long will that be?' Helmut asked.

I finished my seafood and mulled over his question. 'Depends on your cooperation in the matter,' I said defiantly.

'Or my non-cooperation,' he said, munching the last of the prawns swilled down by his wine. He dismissed the dessert menu. 'Coffee?' he asked as an afterthought.

'Yes, why not,' I said and ordered espresso from the hovering waiter who stood in the background just behind our table.

Helmut nodded mutually then it came to his turn to talk. 'Let me see,' he said quietly, 'you know I had an affair with Sheila but I didn't know she was pregnant at the time. That news came later. I didn't put it in the book because I didn't want to sound callous to my reader so early on. You can surely see that?'

'I can…but that is not a Memoir…only the truth will do for the avid reader, good or bad. You should have told it straight, otherwise it is fiction.'

'I signed a three-book deal. My reader was entitled to hear the truth from the beginning—'

I interrupted, '—they were fobbed off with a half-truth. How many other convenient lies have you omitted from your pages in order to make money?'

'My publisher wanted a best-seller.' he said matter-of-factly. 'Any controversy in the beginning was frowned upon so we skipped over certain points. They wanted to depict a hero of Germany. I obliged them.'

'And that's what they got, as you say, and you distorted the truth because your lavish lifestyle needed maintaining. The image of the perfect non-Jewish German boy caught up in an idealistic propaganda machine then sold the notion that people like you were the future of the world. How wrong can you get?'

'The books have sold well.'

'That in your opinion is justification enough. And the publisher is delighted with the results. I have been on the Internet and you are a global sensation. But there are other factors to be considered as well in your success.'

He was clearly agitated.

'Such as?' he said waspishly, leaning forward to me in a menacing manner.

I did the same thing.

'For a start, you are on a world tour,' I said. 'Secondly, you wrote a bestselling crime thriller before the trilogy was published and it was based on fiction and you still write like this. Fair enough, just don't call it a Memoir. If you are going to tell your Memoirs, tell them straight…'

'And upset my readership?'

'If necessary,' I snorted.

'And my publisher?'

'Especially them! I get it, you have both found riches out of this. But they cannot dictate what they want, even if they have ploughed money in.'

'They can and they do to a certain extent.'

'Then change publisher. Or I can spoil your world tour.'

'Easier said than done. I have signed my rights over. Any court case will take years to complete, and my reputation would be ruined as a result of it!'

'My heart bleeds for you. Then there is the small matter of your celebrity wife…'

'What of Isadora?'

'That she is signed up by the same publisher for a zany take on her TV antics in a book which will be hilarious no doubt. She will have her own followers but with yours in addition she is actively helping you in your exploits in gaining new readers. A win-win situation I say.'

'You have done your research.' Helmut raised his eyebrows.

'I have.'

'It's called clever marketing.'

'Exactly! I don't normally have a problem with this, except it is built on lies…and Isadora looks just like Sheila. Does she know she is a copy of your original love?'

'No.' Then he said: 'Only you know the truth. One bloody reader, and that is you. Ok, three…you, your dad and your grandfather.'

'That is enough…to upset the applecart.'

'Upset the applecart? What does that mean?'

'Damage things basically,' I said.

'And you intend to do that?'

'I just might…depends on the level of cooperation you give. You have already answered this: Does your wife know who she reminds you of?'

'Of course not! Just coincidence, I believe…'

'You've said that before,' I said, and then added, 'hardly gives any confidence…'

'Do you see a likeness?' he enquired.

'I do. More importantly, do you share my view?'

'Now that you come to mention it.…'

'I suddenly do,' I said, finishing his sentence for him.

'Indeed,' I heard him mutter under his breath.

'Yes, indeed,' I echoed loudly so all the customers and staff in earshot were aware of my comment. Our conversation echoed around the walls. I didn't want this hidden. The place was filling up fast. I was fed up with just being an incognito number in the great scheme of things. I wanted him to face facts or I would do it for him by hook or by crook. I didn't much care how he chose. It was my call anyway and I felt strong. He seemed vulnerable. That is why I returned to Venice: I wanted the truth. I couldn't rely on the testament of Albert because of his dementia, which clouded things. My dad wasn't playing ball yet because of his fear of the truth and he wasn't feeling well either.

Would Helmut? He seemed to be my only chance.

I said to him directly, 'So are you going to tell the whole truthful story or just a fantasy version to help keep your avid followers and your good wife happy?'

'Good wife?' he laughed incredulously. 'Is that what you think?' Then he changed tack. 'Will you interfere and tell Isadora my past?'

'Yes,' I said. 'She is entitled to hear the real events…from you or me.'

'And…that would be what, to be precise? We all have a past.'

'But not bound in print. You got a British girl probably pregnant in England, and ran back home at the first chance that presented itself.'

'Is that what you think happened?'

'Yes. That you had an affair with Sheila in England just as war was about to break out. How convenient for you. You hid the truth behind the aspirations of your own father. The cowardly deeds of the boy who ran back home and expected the poor pregnant Lincolnshire girl to run to Munich after you was forgotten…now that would have been worth writing about but you and the publisher wanted a hero to cheer during very difficult times in the country of your birth. It helped to lift spirits among people. She stayed in England, showed loyalty and did the decent thing and married Albert, and had a child by whoever and defied your ultimatums. Some girl, eh?'

'I've never forgotten her.'

'But you hadn't really forgiven her either.'

'I had my own family to consider later. I had to move on,' he yelped.

I wasn't fooled by him. 'Yes, there was that… the need to protect them from the lies you first instilled in them. After all, you were the perfect family or so you told "everyone" in your books.' Your affair with my grandmother was too sordid to talk about, and you had to be patriotic. That's how it worked.'

'Except in your interpretation, of course. Are you threatening me?'

'It was bound to happen. You have promoted your memoirs across America to Singapore but it took a simple man like me to come here on your doorstep to unravel the puzzle. You spoke first on the subject, and I was just a spectator who asked too many questions after. And yes, I am threatening you.'

'You could say that.' He shrugged. 'I was expecting you anyway and I am taking your threat seriously. Very seriously. I could have you eliminated.'

That last observation worried me. He could have me killed, and avoid interrogation. I was so close and yet so far. I preferred being so far (and probably saving my life in the process), but then I would never have met Sonia.

Was this a poisoned chalice? Perhaps I was getting close. The daggers were out.

'Tell me, did we meet by accident or did you orchestrate the whole damn meeting between us?' I asked.

'It was when I first heard your name.'

'From Norman?'

'Yes, we were discussing things during one of our weekly chats.'

'You know Norman?'

'I know everyone in this region,' he said smugly.

'And my name just happened to come up.'

He laughed. 'Something like that! I told you I have been here forty odd years and I know everyone's business. I knew Norman, courtesy of Godfrey, very well and we were just chatting about art…and your surname came up and I made connection. Simple as that. You were on his register to rent his house.'

'Not as simple as that, surely?'

'Well, no, but a surname like yours tends to stick. What I didn't know was who I was meeting, my possible son or my possible grandson, or neither. I did my research on the Internet and arranged our meeting…coincidentally. I only say this because we could have easily missed one another.'

'You like your coincidences…why didn't you just give me a wide berth during my time here?' I implored.

'Curiosity, and I couldn't take the chance and I knew you would meet Godfrey on business at some point and he can be a blabbermouth, especially after a drink or two. I wasn't risking my hard-fought reputation after all these years.'

'So you stalked me.'

'You could say that. Are you flattered?'

'Should I be?'

'Sonia thinks so, but thank you for heeding my warning,' Helmut said.

I shuffled nervously, admitting: 'I didn't.' Then I said, 'Where is she?'

'Gone back to Rome to study. Are you going to see her and defy me?'

'What? And reveal the truth to her as well? Is that what you want?' I was incensed.

'No need.'

'You are very flippant. We could be related. Have you thought about that aspect or have you planned for that as well to protect your image?'

'It occupied all my thoughts. But, as I said, no need. I…and you and Sonia…are protected because the truth is your dad belongs to Albert and Sheila, not me and Sheila.'

'Are you absolutely sure of that?'

'Reasonably.'

'That is not an answer to satisfy the dire circumstances! Why then do you object to Sonia and I getting close?'

'Twofold: first, you could be related. I said "reasonably". And secondly, I don't want complications for her. Remember, she has a divorce to finalise and she is very fragile. You are also married. I also want to avoid any unsavoury digging by the press.'

'Makes sense. Keep the current machine well oiled. How do you know of my private life by the way?'

'I have the necessary contacts.'

'OK, I get that. I feel a little vulnerable. I am going through a divorce as well. Things could get messy, so timing could be an issue. And, in your opinion, I am not reliable, which I have to agree with! Why did Albert chase you around Europe during the war?'

'I don't know. He obviously thought I was the father to the baby Sheila brought into this world. She didn't know the answer to his question. He wanted revenge of some kind. She just wanted normality, I represented abnormality.'

'How did you get the war wound?' I said, raising my hand to the sky in recognition of his distorted fingers.

Helmut looked at his hand and then at me. 'Haven't you read about this specific episode in book two?' he asked.

'That's the trouble,' I commented. 'What can we believe? You also mentioned Isadora earlier in very unkind words. Why?'

'That is a different story,' he said coldly.

Chapter Ten

Back in the comfort of my hotel room (I couldn't rebook Norman's place at such short notice and it was expensive as well), I reread the episode in his book of the hand shooting, and didn't believe a word he had written. It was all just propaganda, although described in a compelling manner. I was hooked and I suppose that is what was intended…Helmut could certainly tell a strong story and convince the reader that he was writing just what had happened to him. Shot in action on the frontline? Here comes the hero again. Bullshit!

Very doubtful. Every reader was sucked in, except me. I saw the fiction. Bloody good writing, but wrong in reality, I reckoned.

According to this chapter, Helmut was shot through the shooting hand at close quarters during fighting the enemy face to face in Poland in 1940 against resistance fighters. Not so. It sounds good, but any serious wound like this would have rendered him useless to actually fighting the following war effort. Instead, he would have had a desk job. He would have no further active duty on the western front conquering all of Europe as he would like us to believe.

Yes, the history of his regiment was there for all to see, but it never mentioned anyone by name. He used nicknames. So he could have made it all up and put himself in all the heroic situations, which he did…to sell books, and enhance his own role he played by bulldozing over France and their big goal, the capture of an Island called Great Britain, which they never achieved in getting. Until their defeat and eventual retreat Helmut kept his head above water and portrayed the perfect German soldier, and then eventual commander, which was a stylised version of what his nation, in particular, wanted the hero to be. He told his story well from past experience as a best-selling author, and we bought into his version.

Albert knew the reality, but could he remember it clearly before senility or death overtook him? I was determined to ask Albert his version of what happened when they did finally meet, probably at the end of the war in Italy.

How poetic.

I said to Helmut, 'So have the DNA test if you are so confident.'

'And ruin my marriage? I'm in enough trouble with her as it is.'

'Firstly, she doesn't need to know; secondly, we only need my dad to cooperate alongside Albert which will eliminate your need; thirdly, why are you in trouble with Isadora considering she wants and needs your large readership around the globe? Are you telling me your marriage is in trouble?'

'It might be, but I don't want her suspicious of a DNA test. My doctor tells her everything so I can't just have a smear done without her knowledge and—'

'What about client confidentially?' I interjected.

'No such thing at my advanced age, you cannot even fart without her knowing. Remember she is the region's adopted daughter and a heroine to the people of Venice. She keeps an eye on me…wherever I go.'

'What about another doctor or clinic?'

'I suppose so, London perhaps or Munich, but certainly not here, as word travels fast and I would have to explain my actions.'

'And you are not prepared to do that?'

'No. Not here anyway, my wife is too important in Italy, especially Venice. She is more important than me here. So there is a need to tread carefully.'

'Are you afraid of your wife?'

'Yes.'

'Does she know too much?'

'Like all wives…she knows too much. Too much to gain, too much to lose…depending on her viewpoint.'

I was bemused. He was elderly, so I had to tread carefully. 'Enough to damage you?'

'Yes,' he said again. 'Just like you, my friend.'

'I am not your friend. She needs you.'

He shrugged his shoulders. 'For now…'

I asked the loaded question: 'Is Isadora having an affair?'

'I believe so.'

I was surprised by his swift response.

'With whom?' I asked intrusively and speedily.

He shrugged again. 'Does it matter? My wife and I are different ages. Firstly, I am elderly and dying. Secondly, she has physical needs. I am impotent and will be dead soon.'

'And that is good enough for you?'

'Secrecy protects my image. This is all I crave at my age.'

'And that is vital to you?'

'Yes. You wait until you're my age, then you will understand better.'

'If you are correct in your analysis about dad, then why organise a meeting with me?'

'Curiosity, I suppose, as I said earlier. I wanted to see what might have happened. What might have been to my life.'

'Not a lot,' I observed, trying to bring a big smile to the scenario.

Instead, he smiled thinly. 'Your surname brought back memories for me. For all I knew, I was meeting your dad. Age was not mentioned. Why would it?'

I pondered this, and then asked: 'Have you a good or bad marriage then?'

'In the circumstances, yes it is fine as long as I turn a blind eye.'

I looked at him, slightly puzzled. 'Who is she having an affair with then? Can you give me a name?'

Helmut shocked me with his reply. 'Godfrey, of course. How can he do this after what I have done for him? He was in my inner circle, as Isabel is. She obviously imparted delicate information to him.'

'Why should she do that?'

'Because I was cruel to her. I have a cruel streak in me.'

Of course, I thought.

Then he shocked me even more.

'Were you thinking of someone else?' he asked politely.

I didn't know what to say, so I kept quiet.

I was still dumbfounded with his first answer, to be honest with you. It might seem obvious to you, but I was caught at the wicket, first ball.

Chapter Eleven

We continued our tense conversation.

'Albert said you were a bastard,' I said. 'Why did he call you that?'

'Because…I suppose I was. I stole his girlfriend,' Helmut replied. There was a long further silence between us.

'Are you going to elaborate?' I asked eventually, still thinking of the elderly artist impregnating Isadora. I shuddered at the prospect. Wouldn't you? The beauty and the beast conjured up an unlikely image.

'What? And incriminate my past?' Helmut replied.

'You already have,' I accused him. 'With your books.'

'Ha ha, very funny,' he added. 'My publisher would hardly agree with that assessment with the money rolling in.'

'You only need one voice to shout…'

'Oh, and you intend to be that voice? As if we haven't had any dissidents before. We will surely squash you like the others down the years. The bandwagon rolls on.'

'No previous dissent that really matters, but what with our type of authority at our fingertips, we can create a lot of problems for you.'

'Mister Snow, how much money do you want to keep your silence?'

That was a new one on me and for a second I was figuring out a deal. Typical of my way of thinking, but I was not in the gallery back home. Money was not a consideration right now. Albert and Helmut would be dead soon. But I needed the truth of my past, to be honest with you. I could get that from the horse's mouth before it was too late. But time was at a premium for both of them. I felt sick at this prospect of losing Albert, in particular.

'No money,' I said.

'Nothing?' Helmut raised his eyebrows and stared deep through me, making me squirm uneasily on my chair. 'Then you seek the truth after all. It goes no further than this?'

I thought of everyone, especially Sonia. 'It need not go any further unless you alter lives. Then we have a problem.'

'We all have a problem,' Helmut muttered under his breath, and then he began. I listened, transfixed, like I was watching a man dig his own grave and I was the only witness to this gruesome task.

ooo

Let us go over old ground once again. Helmut came to England aged around eighteen and went back to Germany in 1938 and served in the army. During that period, his father did well as a rep across northern Europe but the rise of Hitler proved irresistible to the head of the family who wanted to leave his own mark on the world. Ironic that Helmut's dad was refused on health grounds to fight on Polish soil and it was the eldest son of two who soon made his stamp of recognition on the German advance army. This part was true, I hasten to add.

Whilst in England, Helmut had an affair with Sheila O'Dowd, my grandmother from Irish descent. She at the time was dating Albert Snow and they all worked together on a farm, mainly at weekends with the same group of kids from the area. An idyllic existence…about to be torn apart by an obscene obsession of one man back in Germany. Trouble was, Hitler had a lot of angry followers from a largely disenchanted country. Unemployment was high and they worshipped everything Hitler stood for. The Nazi party was on the warpath.

It was known that Sheila (a beautiful girl who turned heads) and Albert were an item, but a good-looking German lad got between them, and this German lad knew his destiny in life. And that was not in Lincolnshire as an internee during the next six years after Britain declared war on Germany. Mostly ignorant of his growing reputation as a ladies' man, he was not to know this at the time, but word got around fast that a local lass had got pregnant and suspicious eyes looked at Helmut as the dad.

Suddenly, this foreign family was gone…and that was that. Everyone soon forgot them, except Sheila and Albert. The reason? Sheila was the girl who got pregnant and she insisted that Albert was the daddy, although having a second name in German cast a huge black cloud over the neighbourhood gossip, especially as the marriage of Albert and Sheila was put together so rapidly. The birth of Alec came soon after. Tongues wagged. So why Dieter as a middle name? It was bound to cause friction. Not according to Sheila, who apparently wanted to pay homage to a friend of sorts. Nobody bought into this unsurprisingly. The name was quickly changed to Derek for birth certificate purposes, etc. Was there an ultimatum from Helmut to Sheila before he departed for home?

Helmut shook his head vehemently: Not according to him. The baby was not his. DNA didn't exist then. Sheila and Albert argued. Villagers argued.

The German lad could not defend himself as he was not there on English soil.

Rubbish, I thought, all tosh! We now had the technology to prove a point, but no one was willing to have it, except my poor dad, who had conditions, to discover who my father belonged to. Seemed a reasonable request. It was mainly shameful behaviour in my eyes! Well, let sleeping dogs lie normally and I could see everyone's reluctance so late in the day but I wanted to know who my real grandfather was. I had a right, didn't I? Perhaps I was the problem, after all, I was the only one causing a fuss. So why was I so bloody angry? I knew why.

I could be related to this man. Therefore, I could be related to his daughter, Sonia! And we had not fucked yet but it was on the cards we would if the circumstances were right! Someone had to tell me the truth, and fast, in case we did something illegal. Even if it wasn't, it didn't seem right. Where did I get a moral compass from? Beats me, but I and Sonia had to be comfortable with the scenario. Those ultimately responsible had to act now, before it was too late. I was falling in love with Sonia for my sins, or the sins of others.

Oh, I hear you snigger, three times I have put my 'faith' in female companions and failed. Surely, I wouldn't fail again? Don't bet on it! I was a fool with other women's emotions, especially with those close to home. Was I close to home? You can read on and make your own mind up. I'm just the idiot telling the story. What one does in Venice stays in Venice, I say, thinking of Sonia. I'm very fickle, defying my rights as to the truth of this tale. The truth always hurt someone. I was in the firing line, and it didn't sit comfortably with me.

'Is Godfrey having just the one affair?' I asked.

Helmut began to cry. I had not seen this before. I was stunned.

'I mean, is he having an affair with Sonia as well?' I continued the interrogation, standing on thin ice, it appeared. Seemed reasonable to ask. I wanted to know his 'take' on the situation.

'No, thankfully, but I wouldn't put it past him. Actually, this comment of yours is insulting.' Then he sighed. 'But he will try it, like he does with all his sitters. Some you win…'

'…Some you lose,' I said, finishing his sentence and damning him with the same sentence in regard to Sheila. After all, he was a womaniser as well. He knew it. I deliberately detached myself from his suffering. Wasn't that decent of me? He was now sobbing. I hated crocodile tears. He knew that as well.

Therefore, I was not remorseful to his plight. Once caught, do not let go, is my new motto. Tighten the grip still further.

'It takes two to have an affair,' I said. 'I don't somehow see Sonia falling for his persuasive charms.'

'Oh,' he steamed, 'so my wife did then?'

'You fed me the information, remember?'

He stared at me as if I was dirt on his shoes. Perhaps I was. This was a sore subject.

'Well?' I said.

'Well…it started when I became impotent nearly ten years ago. I lost my 'power', if you get my meaning, and Godfrey took over so to speak during a painting session with her. You've got to remember that Isadora is much younger than I and has her carnal needs and I could not provide them.'

'And Godfrey could even at his age and did so… willingly?'

'Yes.'

'With your permission?'

'Yes.'

'But you spoke earlier as if it was a secret between them?'

'It was, almost. It suited them to keep it secret because he was married as well. An affair is different.'

'Explain yourself.'

'She knew things, I knew things, and I was elderly but we had a good marriage which allowed for certain indiscretions. We had invested wisely and Isadora would carry on and benefit financially if we stayed a true union to the end. I could not deny her this union just because of our age difference. She had put a lot into our relationship. But I have changed my mind if he replaces me and gains wealth that I had created.'

'Sounds utterly reasonable. Is Godfrey therefore a threat to this?'

'Of course. Isadora and I have a pact.'

'So Godfrey was just a sex buddy in the beginning.'

'You could describe it like that.'

'How would you describe it then?'

'Like a toothache, eating away at me. I hadn't factored in jealousy.'

'Your marriage is eroding before your eyes, and then I turn up and spoil things further which questions the validity of your heroic image with the adoring public. About right?'

'About right. First, I want to preserve my marriage. Or I will end the union if this becomes impossible to deal with.'

I wish I had not ignored that last statement. But I did turn the other cheek and continued to use my words as a weapon. 'Anything, it seems, to protect your image whilst you are alive as the great German hero, which must be preserved at all costs to show you in a good light. Is your whiter than white image that important? Everyone else is accountable in some way, except you. Correct?'

'Correct. I have sinned in my life; I know that much. It just snowballed in my writing and my readership demanded more, so I provided it.'

'By telling bigger lies.'

'Yes.'

'Is your publisher involved?'

'Not directly, they just went along with it as long as it made big money.'

'Did you tell lies to your wife as well.'

'Yes, mainly by exaggerating incidents and retelling them in the books.'

'But she knows the truth?'

'Yes.'

'And she has asked for a divorce?'

'Yes.'

'And she can spill the beans as a result of this. I thought you said she would suffer financially?'

'She can, and she will harm her own career along the way. Hardly the case now, what do you think? Currently, she has access to my huge readership around the world. If we stay together. Bingo! This needs protecting. She cannot fail with this if she keeps quiet, and I die a hero in my lifetime. I deserve that. Everyone wins. That is why she will keep quiet. The readership will bring in huge reward for her. Her career is in the ascendancy and growing daily mainly because of her TV work. She is now a national treasure. So any divorce will have to be very secret and undemanding. To do that, she will have to be whiter than white. Or the divorce is forgotten entirely while I am alive. Hence, any affair is forbidden in my view. It has to be buried at the very least while I'm alive.'

'Does your wife know about Sheila?' I probed.

'Yes.'

'Does she know she is the spitting image of my grandmother?'

'Yes, she discovered old photos I had.'

'Does she know I am aware of the likeness? I spilled the beans to her at the home you share.'

'Yes. And it made her ask questions of me too, which was awkward.'

'She questioned the pact.' I thought deeply. 'There is a way out of this,' I said.

'I'll come to London incognito and have a DNA test,' Helmut mumbled.

'Or just tell the truth,' I implored.

'I have, as best I could. It was nearly eighty odd years ago…I honestly can't recall what happened exactly in Lincolnshire.'

'Bullshit,' I said, 'you remember everything! When are you coming over?'

'Oh, I don't know.' He checked his pocket diary. 'In about three weeks, I have an opportunity to come over to London for a few days on my own. I'll do it then.'

I thought about this and gave a straight answer.

'You could be dead by then,' I remarked dryly, but it was a pertinent observation. We could all be dead by then. That would solve things!

He never answered this point and to be honest with you, I never expected a response. Helmut was bereft of emotion unless he could write about it…Isadora's demands and my demands simply destroyed his wrongly misplaced confidence in a world he wanted to control until his dying day. His wet eyes suddenly dried up. Now he wanted to protect those closest to him: Sonia, for instance, his one daughter. Very fitting.

I would not tolerate his possible natural death and I vowed to get Albert's version of events before he died too. I had a flight booked for the morning and I wasn't going to get any more sense from my guest anymore. He was spent for now. I suddenly said as an afterthought, 'Do you know Jack and Jill?'

'Yes.'

'Were they your spies checking up on me?'

'Yes, I'm afraid so.'

'Why did you think I needed spying on?'

'I was just—how you say—sussing you out.'

'You could have chosen better than them.'

'Low-life, but needs must!'

'Am I considered low-life as well, Helmut?'

'I will reserve judgment on that point.'

That put me and my family issues into perspective.

'And did I need checking out?' Helmut laughed.

'Absolutely,' I said, without blinking at him.

The battle was on.

Chapter Twelve

What would you do next? I had the night free. See Godfrey or Isadora on my last night and get their version on things? Seemed the obvious thing to do. I phoned Godfrey and scored first time. We arranged to meet in the bar of the hotel Hilton at nine o'clock in the evening on the Island of Giudecca where he lived and worked, as you are aware. I ate alone at my cheaper hotel and waited for the time to pass. We met and I could tell by the smell of alcohol on his breath he had been drinking beforehand. I had a glass of house red which he paid at the end of our meeting and got the barman to refill our glasses with the house merlot as and when. It would have been cheaper to buy a bottle.

There we go. Cheers! I was in one of those moods. The bar was opulent, like the rest of the decor I entered to meet my guest. It felt like being wrapped in furry cotton wool during my stay.

Expensive cotton wool.

'Well,' I said at the allotted time, taking a swig from my glass. I am a stickler for punctuality, if you believe that, then you will believe anything! I got it right only once, when meeting Helmut. Remember?

'Well,' he replied, without looking up from his accompanying newspaper.

Buying me a drink did not excuse this behaviour. I had that effect on people, however. I could speak but remained unseen by others. I broke the ice as only I knew how.

'Godfrey, how nice to speak to you, and thank you for our meeting, Your Highness. I was with Isadora earlier (I lied) and she sends her regards and I left a pile of your dirty underwear next to your front door for you to clean…assuming you do that sort of thing!'

He suddenly looked up and I knew I had caught his attention, big time.

Luckily for him, our surroundings were largely empty of other ears eager to listen in. Only the barman remained in our vicinity and he was busy cleaning the vacated tables in the lounge area. This spot would get busy again as midnight approached.

'Do you intend to talk like this all night?' Godfrey asked brazenly.

'Well, that depends on you. Are you going to carry on reading your bloody newspaper?'

He discarded the newspaper and gave me his full attention. 'How long have you known about her and me?' he nonchalantly asked.

'Long enough,' I sighed. 'Do you eventually intend to marry her?'

'Goodness, no!' He replied playfully. 'I'm too set in my ways and the choice out there is a little tempting when you consider my profession Besides, I am married. Let's say, Isadora and I had an arrangement.'

He smirked at me as only he can do.

I was ruthless. 'Oh, by that, you mean you also indulge in the female young models that pose naked for you in your studio?'

'Exactly. It goes with the territory, you'd be surprised by their lack of security and my velvet tongue. It can work wonders; you just have to know when to push the buttons!'

'And have you pushed the buttons on Sonia yet?'

'Thought you'd ask that…no, I haven't cracked that one yet. Besides, she only has eyes for you. Did you know that?'

'I do. And that is my dilemma to solve.'

'And Helmut is my best client and therefore my dilemma…'

'Yes, but he will be dead soon.'

'True. So will I.'

'And you don't see the financial opportunity to move in?'

'Thought about it, but I am rich anyway. I reckon I can at last distance myself, and be my own boss instead of being owned in this city. Who owns this city…why, Helmut and Isadora of course to a certain extent and I am a bit sick of being at their disposal. I am an artist in my own right with interest coming in from around the globe, but that interest only lasts so long and at my age I need to act now to cement my reputation. That is why I have said 'yes' to you, but this can easily be a 'no' if you push me on certain subjects.'

'So you can operate successfully without his cash and influence?'

'I can, and do. At first they were important clients and helped me get established in Italy. I even knew his first wife. When they came aboard, everybody else did. But let me remind you, I was bloody good and still am. Like them, doors open for me in this place. You just have to be patient, and have the right type of connections. I'm grateful for that at least…not bad for a poor boy from the backstreets of Bermondsey in London. I have done well with my meagre talent on the world stage. I then met his second wife, Isadora. She was delicious. And she posed for me.'

I thought about this: you had to give Godfrey credit. He hadn't just slept his way to the top. And if he did, who was I to criticise him? He had spent a lifetime here. I had spent just five minutes with him and was demanding answers to my intrusive questions. Unreasonable. But still I pushed the perimeters. I was now treading on very thin ground with his words still reverberating in my head.

'Are you going to discard Isadora then?'

Godfrey almost choked on his wine. I paid to refill our empty glasses and the barman came over and thankfully replenished them and then made himself scarce again.

Godfrey stared at me coldly when we were alone. 'I thought you would be told eventually or you would guess: any discarding has been done already by her. Why was I available tonight, therefore, at the drop of a hat?'

He had a point, and I was very surprised that he agreed to meet me. Now I knew why.

'When did you split up?'

'Who needs to know?' he asked sullenly.

'Anything to do with Sonia?'

He stared at me again and took another large gulp of his drink. 'I have painted Sonia before. Every five years or so, I get a new commission.'

'But never in the nude. Was that Helmut's idea, Godfrey?'

'Yes. Semi-nude was confirmed and it was my idea before the onset of age overtook her. She agreed, the whole family agreed. But I suppose jealousy plays a part in this. I am referring to Isadora here.'

'And you lived up to your reputation?'

'Obviously, and I paid the price by being dumped.'

'By the stepmother?'

'Indeed.'

'And Sonia?'

'What of her? She is at university in Rome. I won't see her again until after I have finished the latest commission which she has sat for fully-clothed.'

'Isadora might be available then as a free woman, a wealthy woman as well. Surely you would have considered that point?' A certain scorn came into my voice.

'Or the family would have imploded by then. Isadora is on the verge. As I said, I'm better off pursuing my goals now, rather than waiting on a call from Helmut. More to the point, he has served his purpose down the years ...'

'And she has, it sounds, listening to you. She has served her purpose.'

'I am not crying, as you can see,' Godfrey said. 'Life moves on. So do I. I am married and I intend to stay married to my existing wife, despite my wandering eye.'

I changed the subject. 'Do you know Jack?'

He pondered this. 'Jack Wiltshire? A fine artist when he is sober and that is not often because he likes a drink. He has a show coming up soon in England. He often pops into my studio. Why do you ask?'

'Oh, he borrowed my apartment last time I was over and I saw his work and was impressed. I was thinking of offering an exhibition to him in the spring of the following year. Do you approve?'

He shrugged his shoulders with a frown on his expression.

'Don't bother.' He said sharply.

'Why?'

'Because he is unreliable and is employed mostly by Helmut.'

'Therefore he is…a spy of sorts amongst other things.'

'A bit harsh! But you could say that, Martin. He goes out with a weird girl…'

'Called Jill. I thought you would know her?'

Godfrey thought long and hard before his reply took me by surprise. 'I do. She was too weird for even me, ha ha. She was originally a model for me, did you know? Jack soon claimed her. I didn't, therefore, stand a chance.'

ooo

I packed my overnight bag and left the hotel next morning for the airport. I couldn't wait to get away from certain people fast enough. Anybody would think I was the problem. Venice rumbled on, the world rumbled on and I messed everything up by my persistent nudging. Perhaps Godfrey touched on another truth during our conversation: we were all as weird as Jill. So who did I bump into at the airport? You guessed it.

'Well, fancy seeing you here. Coming or going?' I asked.

Jill smiled at me with a bewildered look. 'Depends. Are you coming or going?'

I told the truth and waved my ticket in her direction.

'Then I am too.'

Should be fun.

I checked out her tight bottom again in figure-hugging jeans, so who was I to argue? Weird fitted everyone, to be honest.

'Where is Jack?' I asked nonchalantly, looking around for him, her constant buddy it seemed.

'Gone to the States for a month.'

'Didn't you want to go?' I said.

'Na, been before and doors didn't open up for me except porn but you can get that by just staying here. Besides, he's dumped me for another woman so I am available and I love London.'

Checking out her 'porn' body, I couldn't really disagree with her opinion.

'Are you a still a spy for Helmut?' I asked rather belatedly, still thinking of her pert backside under her jeans. How shallow was that?

'Not now,' she said, 'I am a free agent on my travels. I just go for the ride and see where it takes me. I have always done that. Go with the flow is my motto.'

Chapter Thirteen

We had a hoot of a time in London. What happened to Sonia? Out of sight, out of mind, it seemed. When would I grow up? They was exciting days (and nights) and sexual and 'weird' came to mind, but I needed to speak to a coherent Albert, easier said than done. But that is what I wanted to achieve.

He was weird at the best of times as well. He would love Jill if he met her! I had to plan discussing things very carefully with him because dad wasn't playing ball at the moment. So I kept my distance and concentrated on the delectable arse of my girlfriend (Is that the correct description or is this term not allowed these days?) in front of me. Well, wouldn't you? Which wasn't a bad way of doing things in my case, and helped me enjoy myself away from the nightmare of impending divorce and keeping a business afloat.

I basically hid away, concentrating on my companion instead all at the same time. It seemed to work in my book. When it ended, it ended! What shall I call her? Certainly, not as a spy. I kept a close eye on her in my company anyway. She was either very clever or 'weird' or perhaps even both, but I was relishing the challenge of her all the same. I felt alive and wanted. Was she using me as well? You are sniggering again.

On the fourth day, I got lucky with my grandfather. Albert was talking, and talking clearly when I visited with my new girlfriend.

'Are you coming in, Jill?' I said, parking up.

'Yeah,' she replied, 'I'm not sitting outside on my own while you garble on. You could be hours.'

We entered the building and went to his room escorted by a male nurse, who observed: 'He has not stopped chatting,' He then added, 'all day long, yap, yap, yap…I hope you can make sense of it. We have enough trouble with Mrs Pritchard from room eight next door…'

We sat by his bed and I dreaded what Jill was about to overhear but on my previous visit, he was subdued and I was grateful for his quietness but now I was not so sure. I was getting nervous. Anyway, we were here and if I was not to be wary of Jill then this was the occasion. So far, she was fabulous company for an old fool like me. As I have already explained she took me out of my current woes, of which there was plenty coming my way. Maybe Jill was one of them but she made up for any shortfalls with that perfect figure.

At my situation in life, can you blame me for being so short-sighted? Time would surely tell. Why was everybody so laid back? Jack's loss was possibly my gain I surmised. I returned to the harsh reality. My brain was on overload. I was sinking fast. Was all this too much for me? I reckon it was.

'How are you, Albert?' I asked in a whisper, leaning over him.

'Not bad,' he answered, then opened his eyes fully and stared at my female companion. 'Who is she? Never seen her before. Another of your wives or a spy for the soldiers in the basement? Or a whore.'

I ignored his last observation. 'Basement? This property does not have a basement,' I countered.

I was confused by his odd comment. He was hallucinating again.

Albert was on a roll and would not be side-tracked. 'That's what they want you to believe. But I've seen it. Bloody filled with German soldiers ready to take over and steal my jeep, but I'm ready for them …the bastards!' He sat up and grabbed my arm. I was even more perplexed. Overwhelmed, actually. It was going to be one of those nights, I feared.

Albert screamed: 'Call the barracks and have her arrested. Now!'

'Who? Jill? She is with me,' I countered.

'Are you married to her?'

'No,' I said.

'Then she must be a spy for the enemy. Just check with those in the basement. They need shooting, the lot of them, before they run amok. She is one of them!'

'And they will steal your jeep if given a chance,' I added with a smile. Big mistake: the smile.

'And we don't need your smirk!' he shouted in my direction. 'Who is your new friend in Venice? Oh yes, Helmut. Damn Nazi. Wish I could get out of here and hunt him down.'

'Hunt him down?' I said. 'Why? The war ended over seventy-five years ago.'

'Did it? For veterans like us, the war never ended. We won but who actually won? Only death will separate us in the end. There is not many of us left to tell the tale.'

'To tell what?' I asked earnestly.

Albert sat up and came closer to me and whispered, 'To tell it how it happened in reality.'

'How did it happen then?' I asked in the same vein.

'Do we need her here?' Albert said, and pointed a bony finger at Jill.

'Not if you don't want her to stay,' I said in her defence. Perhaps he was in reveal mode and he knew a lot more than me. I felt so vulnerable at this stage.

What was he going to say? I shuddered at the thought, but that was why I was here. Luckily, Jill saw my unease and hovered by the door.

'I'm going for a fag outside,' she muttered. 'I'll be five minutes or you call me when you are finished.' With that comment, she vanished from sight.

Some spy, eh.

'Are we alone?' Albert asked, looking around the room devoid of people except me.

'Yep,' I confirmed.

'Well, just be quiet while I get in the jeep just in case we need a quick getaway,' he said, and got out of bed slowly and sat in an armchair near the window overlooking the carpark. I moved as well, and saw Jill's shadow under the parking light outside strike up a cigarette. I turned to Albert for any pearls of wisdom.

'Climb in and sit beside me,' he ordered.

I did as I was told. I pulled a chair over and sat down next to him.

'Now load up the gun at the front and prepare for a heavy ride out of here.'

I didn't dare disagree with him and did as I was told, pretending to load up an imaginary gun. After all, he was the boss. Truly mad, but still the boss.

ooo

'Get what you wanted?' Jill asked unconvincingly.

I looked at her standing next to the car putting out her second or third fag by crushing the butt under foot. Waiting patiently was not her thing.

'Not really,' I said dejectedly. 'I'll try again, and soon.' I searched for the car keys in my pockets. I was somewhat morose.

'I'm starving,' Jill said, 'shall we get a KFC on the way home? There is one on the corner near the roundabout.'

'Whatever,' I replied glumly. I was in one of those moods. Nothing could shake it off, not tonight anyway. Certainly not a KFC.

ooo

When we eventually got home, I listened to the messages left on the phone machine in the hallway. Big mistake.

'Who is Sonia?' Jill asked. 'Is that the same Sonia from Venice?'

Oh, shit. Jill had overheard the metallic messages and was obviously peeved by this one in particular. Who wouldn't be by the nature of the message. I was cornered.

I said, 'Yes. She is over in London for a few days…'

'Does she intend seeing you? From the sound of things, she does.'

'I will see her, naturally.'

'What about me? Shall I make myself vanish again?'

'That would be good, although a fag or two will not cover our time together.'

Why did my insecurity suddenly come to the surface and spoil things? It was called frustration.

'So I gather,' she said, gesticulating to the bloody machine with a poke of her finger. 'Assuming I'll stick around for the great reunion.'

I couldn't answer that without getting myself in further trouble.

ooo

Next day, while I was in the shower, Jill packed her things and left. Gone, without a word! I was relieved, to be honest with you. A chapter closed sadly.

We had outstayed our use to each other, which was sex and more sex and more sex, I reckoned.

Jill would be missed and as I said we had a hoot of a time together (except the bloody KFC!). But all good things come to an end in the great scheme of things in life. There we go, I could hear her and you say. Exactly my sentiments, to be brutally honest with you.

I wanted to see Sonia while in London for a few days and Jill would undoubtedly have got in the way. I contacted Sonia by mobile at her hotel in central Oxford Street and was eventually put through to her room.

'How long are you here for?' I asked excitedly.

'Three days,' she replied, 'but then again, you should know this from my message to you if you had listened properly.' Her tone of voice was now indignant.

What had I done wrong? In her view, it was clear. In my view, I was just being polite, but she had a point. I was contrite in my reply.

'I'm sorry, I was slightly side-tracked…'

'Obviously.'

I was now damaged goods and I had to redeem myself—and fast.

'Can I see you tonight for food?'

'Well, I have to eat…when and where?' she demanded of me and I had to think fast.

'How about I pick you up at seven o'clock and we eat locally nearby? Do you like Chinese?'

'Yes and yes is the answer. Are you working during the day?'

I responded: 'Someone has to earn the corn. I wish I was with you. What are you doing?'

'Oh, visiting a Museum or walking the Serpentine depending on the weather. What do you advise?' Luckily, she had thawed.

'Sunshine today; rain tomorrow,' I said matter-of-factly, 'so a riverside walk is better suited today.'

'I'm impressed. Hyde Park it is then. Are you working close by?'

'Fairly close. But I must open today as I have an important client calling in but he won't tie himself down with a time. If I do well with him, I can be free the following day.'

'Well, you'd better get in and nail him then!' Sonia said, laughing. 'I want a day with you before I return to Rome and further study. Have we a date?'

'Yep, we have another date! See you tonight?'

'At seven,' she said and put the phone down on me.

'At seven,' I said to no one in particular down a dead line. Then I listened to her message again. Her voice was radiant on the machine. Why wouldn't it be? I encouraged our meeting. Why was I nervous then of seeing her tonight?

She somehow scared me if our relationship was now on a new footing. Jill slipped out of my mind. Does that not surprise you? Especially as Lillian phoned and my brain got even more frazzled. I hated arguments. Why did women have that effect on me? I answered my mobile with a joyous "Hi".

Then I awaited the latest bombardment from my estranged wife. Happy days!

Chapter Fourteen

I managed to see my client at the gallery, a Russian, at lunchtime and, unlike me after talking (mainly listening) to my estranged wife, he was in a generous mood and spent nineteen thousand pounds with me which made my earlier purchase of a ploughman's sandwich a bit more exciting and I looked forward to my Chinese meal even more. At least on this occasion, I could afford it.

Even at West End prices. I relaxed a little. Just. When a divorce is imminent, it is impossible to switch off. I know of people who can relate to that. When was I going to learn the error of my ways? Three marriages, three divorces. Not something to be proud of.

At six-thirty, I closed the gallery and had a stiff brandy, the bottle hidden in my desk. I had had a decent day and sealed another sale at six so it was worth staying open after hours. I had another brandy to celebrate my good fortune.

Then I headed for the Cumberland Hotel near Oxford Street by my car for my date. Oh dear, I hear you mock me. Fortunate for me, I parked close-by. I didn't know how I would be received actually. Some joke, and Jill was absent fortunately. Lucky her, I say. Sit tight while we go on a ride of a lifetime!

At just before seven I entered into the foyer and Sonia was waiting for me at the bar. I ordered a gin and tonic to match her drink (was this a wise move mixing my drinks?) and greeted her with a mouth kiss and big hug. It had been a sunny day, as I predicted earlier on the phone.

'We are running late,' she snapped.

I ignored this remark. I had to calm things down fairly quickly.

'Did you do the Serpentine?' I asked hurriedly.

'Yes, it was wonderful. Did you have a good day?' She was by now all smiles, thankfully.

'I did,' I replied eagerly.

'Did your client show up?

'He did and spent a lot of money with me, so we can celebrate.' I smiled saying this.

I was hungry for food and hoped she was as well. She was.

We emptied our glasses sharply and moved on hand in hand (what was I supposed to do?) down the street but I was still nervous: Albert occupied my mind. Lillian occupied my mind. Jill invaded my mind! But mainly, I couldn't shake off what Albert didn't reveal, and his reluctance or insanity showed brazenly on my open face. At least I could now load an imaginary gun, ha ha. I was preoccupied with my time with Albert. Sonia didn't deserve this deceit of silence from me. I continued nevertheless to be troubled by him and his ranting.

After a delicious meal in a restaurant we walked to near the American Embassy, and she was the first to break the ice: 'So, what's the problem?'

I sat down one a bench with her and looked straight in her eyes and said bluntly, 'We could be related.'

That ruined our romantic time for two.

'How do you work that out, clever clogs?' She asked in a bemused tone.

'Because Helmut might be my grandfather, but I'm investigating this and will know the truth soon, I hope.'

'Bloody Hell.'

'Exactly.'

'We just kissed.' Sonia now looked shocked and vacant.

'Not appropriate in the current circumstances, but it might be. I'm hoping I am wrong in my assumption.'

'Are we related? This is weird. I am in a state of bewilderment. Have you suggested a DNA test?'

I shook my head in desperation. 'Easier said than done!' I thought of the words already spoken by the four of us, Helmut, me and dad and Albert.

Difficult words.

My companion on the bench appeared perplexed. 'You could be German then by blood. What do you think of that?'

I was equally perplexed. When you love someone you don't want to think of the alternative scenario, but we had to consider all options, however unpalatable.

'I want you to meet someone…' I said.

'Who?'

'My grandfather, Albert.'

'Your supposed grandfather,' she corrected me. 'Does this possible outcome affect our relationship?' Her question was loaded with insecurity. She continued, 'I will always love you in any capacity, if that puts your mind at rest. I am angry though, if my father has lied to deliberately distort the past.'

'He might have,' I replied sheepishly, leaving my brain muddled as well.

'What do you know that I don't?' Sonia said with rage.

'Just meet Albert and then you can decide on our future…and perhaps you can talk with your stepmother and father, who are running rings around me so I don't know where I am with anyone.' For once I was being truthful. It hurt even more than telling possible false stories.

'Do we have a future as a couple?' she asked forlornly.

'I don't honestly know…it depends on what we learn,' I said, ordering coffee from a cafe across the road. Sonia sat in silence glaring at the bland walls. I know, I know: I am in a fix, put there by my big mouth. I can't help it.

Abnormal lies and intended silence will always win through whenever the prize stares you in the face. I don't do normal, unfortunately. And Sonia was a prize worth having. If only I could keep my trap shut or ignore assumptions that were not of my making. I was stirring up a great big complex pot, that I didn't know existed when I went to Venice. It consumed me. That's why I was apprehensive. Or terrified.

ooo

I took an unexpected phone call on my mobile.

'Martin, this is your dad. Albert is talking sense and wants to see you at the home. Where are you?'

I stared at my mobile and then at Sonia. I was both elated and sad at the news. 'Are you with him?' I asked.

'Yes. Where are you at present?'

Trouble always seemed to follow me around. 'In central London, I reckon we can be there in about forty minutes…'

'We?'

'Yes, we, and I don't mean Jill.'

'Whatever! Get here as soon as you can,' dad said quickly, and clicked off, with me glaring at my dinner guest. I was at a loss what to say. We had a chance to get to the bottom of the story, but it might be the end for me and Sonia. Someone would get hurt if my possible grandfather remembered events as they happened over eighty years ago correctly so we could believe him at last. He knew the truth. Because he lived it.

We got to the car pretty fast. There was no going back on this one. For everyone.

Forty-five minutes later, we pulled into the Care Home carpark in Carshalton.

'Are you ready for this?' I said, turning off the ignition.

'Are you?' came the stark reply from Sonia.

I didn't answer her and we walked silently to reception. What a night we were having, so far. I checked my watch. It was still early evening to make things seem a whole lot worse. My feet seemed to drag across the tarmac at this point. What else could invade this night? There was plenty of time on the clock. I didn't know whether to laugh or cry.

ooo

'Hi Albert. You wanted to see me?' I said tentatively on entering his bedroom.

'Yes. Who is that?' He asked, pointing to the woman who followed me in.

I looked around. 'Sonia,' I announced confidently.

'Another whore,' Albert said accusingly. 'Every time I see you, there is another strange girl on your arm.'

'Last time the girl was described as a spy by you, but there you go. Shall we sit in your jeep?' I observed wryly, pointing to the chair in the window bay.

'What jeep?' Albert said in a dismissive tone. Then he swore.

I took his point of view. He was in no mood for ridicule by me although I ignored his other offensive remark.

Instead I said, 'This is the daughter of Helmut. We have come to hear your version of what really happened back then.'

'What type of girl am I?' Sonia asked in puzzlement.

Luckily for me, she was ignored by Albert.

'Welcome, Sonia,' Albert said, 'and forgive my language. I didn't know Helmut had a daughter…'

Sonia nodded to him.

'Do you have any relatives alive, beside your father?' Albert enquired.

'No. My father's brother, who was a reputed art historian, died nearly five years ago in an accident in Munich,' Sonia replied.

'And how old are you?' Albert said in ungallant fashion.

I cringed at his direct manner.

'A girl shouldn't normally answer but as we are after the truth tonight… so,

I'm now roughly forty-four if that helps…'

'Who is your mother?'

'Helmut's first wife, Claudia. He is now married to my stepmom, Isadora. I study economics in Rome. I was a very late addition to the family. Anything else you want to know? Oh, by the way, I am not a whore as you suggested.'

'Forgive my bad and inaccurate manners,' Albert said, shifting his fragile weight in the bed.

A nurse popped in. 'Just to let you know,' she said, 'only half an hour left for visitors.'

I took over hurriedly. 'You wanted to speak to me urgently?'

'Yes,' Albert said.

'Well, we have rushed over.'

'I thought I was a little crazy when we last spoke…'

'You were. Are you any clearer now?' I tried to keep calm in the circumstances. We now had under thirty minutes!

Then he miraculously started. We sat gape-mouthed and listened intently without appearing to breath. Try it. Not easy, but manageable if one so relies on the uninterrupted 'spoken word' in under half an hour. None of us dared to speak during his 'recollection'.

'In 1936 we were happy and in love, that is, me and Sheila until a certain young German lad joined our group on the farm. He was great fun and shone his optimistic influence on everyone and I think he stole her heart. I was the shy type. I knew there was trouble brewing over in Germany and our countries tried unsuccessfully to come to some kind of peace. Helmut talked of his family returning home to fight for the Fuhrer. Something like that. They as a family had to beat internment first. Then Sheila got pregnant.

We were all about twenty at the time and Sheila didn't know who the real father was. We argued over her unfaithful nature. However, we both wanted to be the father and Helmut gave her an ultimatum: either return to Germany where he would look after her and his so-called 'baby' in relative luxury or have a life in poverty over here with me and suffer the consequences. He was that confident. Never considered the consequences of bringing a British girl home! Smug bastard.

Obviously, he had an inkling of the 'future' and wanted to plan for it. I had other ideas. He was so arrogant and clearly saw a brave new world on the horizon. She was obviously scared at such a young age for a giant leap of faith to go with him. Instead, we married in England where she was used to living and brought up your father as our own in the community even though Sheila did not know the real donor and insisted on a German middle name in recognition of his possible lineage. I did not agree, but Sheila was adamant at the time. She was so strong, she would have defied a firing squad, if need be.

I went to war in 1939, and whenever we argued, she would taunt me about your father's real dad, although I brought Alec up as my own.

During the war years, I somehow survived and Alec's birth and true father obviously rankled with me and I vowed to find Helmut and discover the truth of parentage if at all there needed to be one. After all, I raised him as my own through thick and thin. But still it rankled! It was a hard task finding him.

When I was in Africa, he served in France. When I got to Paris, he was in Austria. Our paths never seemed to cross until Italy in 1945, at the end of the war, when the German forces finally retreated defeated and Hitler committed suicide. We met eventually in Florence and came face to face at a makeshift hospital in the last days as they surrendered. Did you know that more people were killed during the retreat than in the actual war itself?

Rarely mentioned, but the Germen troops on their return were ordered to massacre everything that got in their way. Everyone, women and children included, were butchered and nobody was exempt. I was recovering from a broken leg in Florence at the hospital when Helmut's unit chanced upon us.

We were dead folk, defenceless against any attack. Luckily for me, I was on the top floor when all below were shot dead. I could hear my comrades being killed and braced myself for the inevitable. Then Helmut appeared and saved me by first recognising my features and then pushing my trolley into a side room for safety. Everyone else was not spared, except me. Helmut was in charge and his troops believed him when he said the top floor was searched and cleared. I miraculously lived on in my hiding place.

Helmut came back to see me and I realised then that the boy, now a man, had in fact spared me from certain death. I thanked him, even though I was terrified of what he could do to an unarmed soldier. I was at his mercy. Instead, he cried. I learnt from him that his own father was refused an army role on unfit medical grounds and Helmut willingly joined up back home to effectively take his place for world domination, which they saw as their natural right. Only the United Kingdom defied them, because we were an Island and difficult to enter and we won the air fight against the odds, and unlike their mainland invasion of other countries which was easier to conquer and hold, like France, for instance.'

'What about the invasion of the Channel Isles then?' Sonia asked.

A fair point.

'Hardly a comparison, dear. We were a different breed and were on the offensive until the end and backed by the yanks so the Germans were depleted and worn out. They had in nineteen forty-one failed to invade Russia, and lost to us a year later in The Battle of Britain. Until then, they thought themselves invincible. They were not. Now they were deflated. The rot began to set in.'

'Just like us, they were basically worn out?' I hinted.

'Very true. But we masked it better and the Battle of Britain saw us through and destroyed German morale. Let us simplify things. They basically retreated from us whilst they recuperated after that defeat and tried to invade Russia again and failed at that as well…the propaganda machine began to grind to a halt. The rest of Europe caved in easily. We were made of sterner stuff (just) and we were an island. Germany had no choice than to retreat in the end but could still cause carnage on their withdrawal, which they did big time.'

'And my father was privy to this?' Sonia said, bleary-eyed.

'As a Commanding Officer, yes.'

'So, according to your version, he gave the orders to kill everyone in the hospital,' Sonia said again.

'Worse…he led the assault, although assault is hardly the correct term,' Albert explained. 'We were sitting ducks, unable to fight back. We were in hospital to be patched up. We were largely bedridden. Although on reflection he helped save my life, although I will never forgive him for slaughtering my unarmed comrades. I wish I had died with them in that dark hour.'

'What happened?' I suddenly asked in solemn mood.

We were all transfixed by these gospel words spoken by a war veteran.

Albert looked up at my question and stared into my eyes. 'Helmut on his return to me brought a standard issue English pistol and asked me to kill him for his sins as I saw fit. He handed me the pistol. He had witnessed much massacre, and was traumatised by it. He wanted it ended, and this was his way out. I was there and could do the dirty deed. Believe me, I was tempted! But the use of an English gun proved he planned this, and me killing him by this method would make him a national hero. I was livid. In a moment of lucidity, I shot him in his trigger hand instead thus rendering him no further use on the front line. He was maimed. Although the war appeared over, you never knew what the future held, so I made a decision! I knew my fighting days were over curtesy of a serious leg injury. I knew too that standing before me was your possible grandad and although I had my chance to kill him I couldn't for that very reason. I also had a past with him, mainly good times. I was torn. He had saved me. What would you do in the same circumstances?

I wounded him. Later we learnt Hitler had committed suicide in his bunker leaving Germany to officially surrender to allied countries. Our war with Germany was over and I eventually returned to Lincolnshire to Sheila and a damaged marriage awaited me. I raised Alec as my own, without any interference.' He looked at my dad. 'I revealed to Sheila about the meeting with Helmut in Florence. She was relieved he was still alive and thanked me for sparing his life. We had two more boys, and all three looked the same…blue-eyed, blond haired with a smile of the devil. Just like me! As you know, two sons have since passed away due to a fatal illness. I mourn them every day I am alive. My wife died ten or more years ago from ill-health and the name of Helmut was never mentioned again thankfully but…here's the thing, you are the only one with a German middle name.'

'Which is?' Sonia asked curiously.

There was a collective pause.

'Dieter,' we all said in unison.

'That's peculiar…' Sonia said to all of us. 'My father's name is Helmut Dieter Grohmann, just to confuse matters. And his brother's name was also Dieter, both named after our great-great grandfather in remembrance. What did the locals make of that?'

Albert shrugged. 'We didn't tell anyone of this name for fear of reprisals…'

'Not anyone?' I asked rather stupidly, looking wide-eyed at dad for a response.

'Not anyone. "D" was always meant for Derek after your uncle so no one called your dad Dieter. We wanted a quiet life.'

'Mum used my middle name,' Alec admitted. 'When she got angry with me, and that confused me as a child.'

'We didn't talk about that,' Albert said, snapping his words with supposed hatred.

Our half hour was up. The nurse saw to that by her presence at the door and our silence that greeted her arrival. We all had a lot to think about.

Chapter Fifteen

I was confounded mainly by Albert's story. He was coherent, that was for sure. The story by Helmut concerning the same period was also surprising to my ears as it contradicted events. So who was right? As we drove home Sonia sat back in her seat and after a period of silence remarked: 'That is fairly easy then. My dad just needs to have a DNA test.'

'Easier said than done,' I replied glibly, fearful of spilling the beans of the so-called affair between her stepmother and Godfrey in Venice which she obviously didn't know about. Or did she? Who was hoodwinking who here…I told you I was confounded. Best to keep quiet on this subject, for the moment.

'Or my dad can undertake the test,' I offered her.

'There is that. Will he?' She stared closely at me.

'He says 'yes' but I think this action is actually a big fat zero,' I snarled. 'He wants things to stay the same, and has largely passed the buck. In his head, Albert is his father.'

'Then who needs to actually know?' Sonia said.

I went very quiet, mulling over the scenario. Seemed pertinent to me in the circumstances with my bold answer. I drew a deep breath and announced:

'I do.'

'Why?'

I looked at her. 'Are you crazy? My grandfather seemed lucid and appeared to tell the truth…'

I stopped the car in a lay-by.

Sonia looked puzzled, then she spoke. 'I wouldn't say otherwise…wait a minute, if Albert is telling the truth then my dad in his memoirs is lying about the past…Is that what you are saying?'

'Exactly,' I said, waiting for the slap across the face.

Luckily for me, it never came.

'Who do you believe?' Sonia asked instead.

Relieved, I answered, 'The war bits? My grandfather sounds plausible but he could talk differently tomorrow! I think Helmut is making a lot of it up to sell books. Parts are missing to make his position look good. The baby? Could be either of them but if my dad is Helmut's then the past has been washed over which is not right and distorts everything, especially for us. For instance, my history is a basic lie. This is then confusing: you and I then have a blood link.'

'Meaning?' she shuddered at the scenario, but surely she had worked it out!

'We maybe cannot have a sexual relationship.' I retorted in my usual crass way, but, accordingly, I was speaking the blunt truth. I might be German and Sonia was related to me. I hated the thought: Sonia related to me just when I had met the perfect woman. Why did I muck around with Jill then? It defied logic but logic stared me defiantly in my face on this occasion. And I always ran from it. Perhaps that was my subconscious fear with women and Jill presented herself at the right time when I was feeling vulnerable. Weak actually. I never said 'no', and that was my problem. I was not reliable. Was it a case of 'out of sight, out of mind'? Probably, coupled with my juvenile brain.

But not on this particular occasion. History could be rewritten…against me.

But at least the truth would be known to all. I almost sound philosophical.

Even I could giggle at this. It was a skill I had perfected down the years.

'It doesn't seem real or fair,' Sonia moaned. 'There is only one cast iron way to find out…a DNA test on either side. Then we will know for sure.'

She sounded suddenly realistic. She had a point. Repeated again, more forceful this time.

'Correct. But my dad is my dad, but at least your father agrees to an overseas test.'

'That is plain ridiculous!'

'Your dad is coming over soon to London then we'll get the answer.'

What else could I say?

'Why not have the test in Venice?' she asked in a bemused manner.

'Because…' and then I lost my nerve. My face turned white.

'Because? What do you know that I don't?' Her voice was indignant and just what I feared. She too turned white as the blood drained from her face as she looked at me solemnly. She was not backing away.

'Speak to your family,' I uttered.

Talk about passing the buck. It was all I could think of saying in my hour of need or desperation. I know, I know…shame on me. Helmut had a lot to answer for. Why should I be his go-between? He created this mess.

'I will,' Sonia replied in despair.

Then we commenced our journey in further silence.

I got in after midnight, exhausted after dropping off Sonia at her hotel. But my phone rang. It was dad.

'What is so wrong to ring this late, dad?' I asked.

'Funny, you didn't have this problem when phoning me from overseas. I've been ringing since eleven and thought you would be in. We need to talk,' I heard him say.

'Well, talk.' It was too late for niceties and I was in a foul mood and just wanted my bed. I was exhausted from talking.

'What did you think?'

'About what…'

'You bloody well know. About Albert's take on things. Why do you think I am ringing about at this time of night? I've been disturbed at this time by you asking silly questions earlier.'

'Morning.'

'What…?'

'It's morning, dad. It's gone midnight…' I was stating the obvious.

'So what! I need to talk…about events of this evening.' He seemed perturbed. I listened with one ear on him and the other somehow attached, so to speak, to my tired eyes longing for my comfy bed. Which would you choose? Him droning on or peace for me between the duvet? I was dead beat and longed for solitude. No chance.

'What do you think?' he persisted.

What do I think? I'm truly confused. 'For a start, I didn't ask silly questions. I'd say on balance, grandfather was lucid tonight and spoke…the truth. Does that make you happier, because it sure hurt Sonia to hear that.'

'Whatever the outcome, Albert will always be considered my father.'

'I get it,' I said this with a misplaced yawn.

'Do you?'

'You don't want German blood in you, so I'm on your side,' I stated.

'Precisely, and all that it entails. Albert is my bloody dad to me, whatever science proves.' My father was angry with this retort to my observation. 'Nor do I for that matter want German blood in me. It complicates things. And Albert will always have a special place in my heart,' he concluded defiantly.

'Just have a bloody DNA test and put us out of our misery,' I wailed.

'We were fine before you went to Venice and met Helmut.'

'No, we were ignorant…'

'But secure in our ignorance.'

'What are you really frightened of?' I asked for the first time.

'I don't want another history,' he replied sternly.

'Even if it's the truth? What about me?' I was quick to add.

'You? You? You have a bloody dad no matter what happens! I want a dad too and he is an Englishman by birth.'

'True, but I was were brought by my real mum and dad and that is not the issue here. I know who are my parents are. Do you?'

'That is cruel. Albert returned from the war and brought me up as his own. That is good enough for me. What my mum Sheila did or not do was her own concern and what she revealed or believed was privy to her and Albert. After all she married him. She even stayed in the community-does that sound like a scorned woman or one on the run from village gossip?'

'Neither, except your middle name is a bit of a giveaway…especially in the circumstances of the matter. Have you never queried that?'

'Of course I have, but always met by a brick wall. I was rarely called that and besides both parents had to approve my full name so it became no big deal.'

'So Dieter somehow became Derek and registered on the Birth Certificate, even if mum in her frustration sometimes referred to you by a German name.'

'Albert dealt with all that.'

'I bet he did. He didn't want too many questions asked or prying eyes looking into his affairs—this was a delicate time for the Country—so everyone came under scrutiny.'

'Especially a dubious dad with a new-born baby and escapees, like Helmut, being connected by gossip,' he said, spitting the words.

'Especially so.'

He suddenly asked strangely, 'Are you alone?'

'Yes. What are you implying?'

'Thought you might be with Sonia?'

'We are not currently talking.'

'Is she annoyed?'

'You could say that…but not necessarily with you or Albert.'

'You then?'

'More to the point!' I said, but quickly corrected myself. 'But more angry with Helmut, her lovely dad who she has just discovered might be a liar and he doesn't care for rocking the boat for other people still alive. Only saving his own skin is the priority, to be brutal in my assessment. By the way, I had a date with Sonia for tomorrow, but this has now been cancelled.'

My father suddenly went quiet, before saying, 'The past has finally caught up with him?'

'You could say that,' I answered. 'Many aspects of odd avenues have opened up which he did not expect to happen.'

'Such as?'

I thought back and pictured Isadora and Godfrey together. 'I'm not at liberty to say right now. Time will tell.'

'Time is not on our side because they are both elderly.'

'On death's door, you could say.'

Then dad shocked me with his next comment:

'About the DNA. I'll have it done immediately, provided Helmut does the same.'

We had been over this before, but this time he sounded adamant.

He continued, 'We cannot ask Albert because that would be obscene. I don't intend to insult him. He deserves a little dignity in his final days on this earth.'

I couldn't disagree.

Chapter Sixteen

What do you say to that? Hallelujah comes to mind! I punch the air with my right fist. Two people now agreeing wholeheartedly to a test. Miracles do happen, in my opinion. I could now live in hope.

Then I slept like a baby, showered when I got up at eight and had breakfast of tea and toast before heading for work, this time on the tube. I was met by Sonia, surprisingly, who was waiting for me at the door at just before nine-thirty. I had told her previously the address of the gallery.

'I'm seeing daddy tonight. He is meeting me at the airport and then we get together later as a family for evening dinner at mum's favourite place.'

'Which is?' It was my time to say something.

'Harry's Bar.'

'Of course,' I said in a throwaway sort of way.

'You don't approve?'

Oh, dear, was I in trouble for expressing that tone?

'Expensive and overrated,' I added anyway.

'Oh, I didn't see you complaining at the Gritti when dad picked up the bill…or was that just forgetful on your part?'

'I tried to pay,' I volunteered.

'Half-heartedly…' She replied, in defence of her father.

I was flummoxed and I didn't want to get into a fight…and lose! I was already on thin ice. 'I was a guest that night and the food was excellent.' I masterfully changed the subject. 'Does Isadora like the famous Bellini then?'

It was an excellent 'get out of jail free' card, thankfully. It altered the conversation between us. Phew!

'Good gosh, no!' Sonia replied. 'They are expensive and overrated, as you say. But she does like to be seen there. Good for the ego for her. Not me. Especially when I get through the famous drink as if they are going out of fashion. Then I become a drunken spectacle for everyone to see, especially to the press in tow. I become a black sheep then.'

'Is she not meeting with you at the airport?'

'No, daddy knows something is up and wants to pump me beforehand, and Isadora is meeting us at the bar later.'

'Later?' I was eager for more.

'She has business to attend to beforehand.'

'With…?' I knew the answer.

'With Godfrey.'

I wish I was a fly on the wall at Harry's Bar tonight. There would be big fireworks on display indoors at the famous restaurant, I reckoned. Or outside!

Wherever. It was sure to happen.

ooo

'Albert? What was the truth last night in your speech?' I asked him.

I knew the nurse on duty last night didn't approve of me grilling again, but what was I supposed to do? I know, grin and bear it! Not my style (ask the ex-wives) and I wanted him today to tell a similar story as the last one to help me substantiate it.

Albert said, 'Where is the girl?'

'She would refer to herself as a woman,' I said with irritation and checked my wristwatch. Too early to be that damn fly with big ears on the wall in the restaurant. Not so big ears apparently. I could pretend to hear Sonia's temper over the cloudy skies as any apparent argument grew louder. Noise apparently travelled fast in these parts. Well, I hoped so. Any ammunition would be useful.

'OK, woman then. Still a spy in my book…like the other one you brought before.'

'You are close,' I joked.

'Where is she?' he asked.

'Which one?

'The woman.'

'In Venice.'

'With her father?'

'With Helmut, yes.'

'How is he?'

'Old,' I joked again, without getting a laugh for the second time. I was also getting restless. 'The story, Albert?'

He told me again, almost word for word which suited me…for now anyway.

'Why is your recollection of the past so clear to you,' I observed, 'when, generally, you can't recall what you did yesterday?'

'I remember Sheila quite clearly, not just a pretty face. Well-rounded, with child-bearing hips. We had history. Plenty of meat to get your hands on, not like the other girl you brought over. She was far too skinny! All bones!'

He was obviously referring to Jill.

'Not your type,' I said dryly.

He ignored me, thankfully. A discussion on the attributes of the fairer sex was more than I could handle right now.

'Can't keep up with you and your active sex life. Time to put the past to rest and any soldier who might not talk of the war today always remembers what went on. Always!' Albert stated plainly.

I wasn't going to argue with that. What did I know with what they had to endure in those years? A haunting comes to mind. They lost dear friends in the battlefield. The horrors. Those that survived still felt guilty for living. I felt out of order just mentioning about it.

'I lost a brother in the war, you know!' Albert continued, tears in his eyes.

'Yes, Dick.'

'Blown up by a bomb he was trying to defuse on the last day of the war! Typical, he died on foreign soil, while I survived and returned home with minimal injury.' Albert frowned. 'Just leg problems for me. No justice.'

'No justice?' I remarked. 'Alec was brought up in the bosom of a loving family…don't forget that! You should be very proud of that achievement.'

Was he?

He reflected. 'I thought so until you put doubts in my mind with all this nonsense sprouting from Helmut's books…well, here's the thing, let him have his ill-gotten glory. After all, we won the war, and I raised your dad as only I knew how—my own way. As far as I was aware, Helmut died on the retreat.

Good riddance! I'm surprised he is still alive. We will all be dead soon and then they can examine this war hero and pick holes in a flawed story or yarn as I would call it. There is no point in being the richest man in the cemetery.

'Someone will benefit from his riches,' I pointed out.

'Ah, you mean the trophy wife! Let her have the money and see how she handles it when the media vultures get at the blatant lies in his story. Have you met her?'

'Yes.'

'Tell me, who does she look like?'

I detected a mischievous side to him.

'Er, Sheila,' I confessed. 'Exactly like in the photo of her you keep beside the bed.' I hesitated. 'They could be twins.'

'Sheila was beautiful. What do you think?'

'Of the likeness? Isadora is beautiful if that is what you are asking me.'

'Typical of him.'

'What?' I asked.

'Of wanting my girl, and failing miserably with a substitute…'

'That's rather harsh. Last time I looked, he had everything going for him,' I commented wryly, not daring to mention Isadora's supposed affair. Seemed the least of my worries. Let Sonia sort that out! I checked the wall clock and did the calculations. Bet she was having fun right now. Albert brought me back to earth with a bang.

'Well, he's not having your dad,' he said defiantly.

I was suddenly alarmed by this rant. Dad joined us in a frenzy as Albert cried out loud again. A nurse joined us and comforted her stricken patient and questioned the wisdom of our visit.

'What the hell happened?' dad raged, as the nurse administered an injection of sedatives to calm Albert down as he tried to fend off any demons surfacing in his brain. 'Well?' was the next bombardment coming from Alec.

'He repeated the story of the past and then got hysterical,' I said rather absurdly.

Dad was confused. 'And you had nothing to do with his behaviour? I come every night since mum died and have never seen him so upset since then…'

I tried to deflect his anger.

'I expected you earlier,' I said feebly.

'I was tired from the phone call with you and wanted a quiet night to reflect on things. Now this!' My dad was clearly angered as he stomped around the room again.

I thought of Sonia again. What was she getting through this evening? Kicking ass, I hoped.

'I had better go,' I said, grabbing my jacket from the back of the door.

'It's for the best,' dad said. 'Albert's old and fragile. We can talk later when we have all calmed down.'

'Righto,' I said, relieved that someone smarter than me was taking over. It was a long drive home alone and I had a lot of thinking to do. Albert's last words kept resounding in my head.

ooo

When I got to the car, my world turned upside down. It was dad unexpectedly on my mobile.

'What's up?' I asked bemused.

'You'd better come back in.'

'Why, is Albert ranting again?'

'Not quite…'

'Well, you can handle it. I seem to cause trouble wherever I go. Shall I come back in and kiss him goodnight. Will that help soothe him?'

'Hardly…'

'Then what do you want me to do?' Just shut up and listen without the verbal diarrhoea for starters, my brain told me.

Alec's voice trembled, even on the phone. 'I'm afraid Albert has passed away.'

'Dead? Are you telling me he is dead?' I was in shock, not talking or thinking straight.

'You must be close by…'

I was still in the fucking carpark to the Care Home! '…then come back in and identify the body with me and cuddle me. I need your comfort as never before.'

Chapter Seventeen

Have you ever seen a corpse?

I have. I was looking at one, not a pretty sight, although I used the word 'angelic' to help soothe dad. I cuddled my dad. Albert died with both anguish and anger on his lips. I was the last person he spoke with. At least I had that, despite dad's sorrow and bewilderment, as the room filled with apparent strangers as they worked hard but pointlessly to revive him.

I knew he was dead and at ninety-eight but he deserved to die on his terms: he had the last word. He was a proud man and a honourable one and had lived his life on his terms as many survivors of The Second World War had. They lived an entirely different time to us. They were stoic men and gained victory on a grand scale which hopefully we would never experience and there was great personal loss as well. But it had to be done at any cost.

Albert was a hero of mine. I don't believe any soldier thought they would live though the war. Those like Albert didn't want to talk and explain themselves as barbaric criminals in the name of duty. They were under orders and did what was necessary. Full stop. The ordinary people back home depended on them for victory. We did what we could to help their campaign on foreign land. We, as a nation, didn't ask the right questions and they never offered an explanation to what was required to obtain success.

But history did, and recorded it as unforgiving and gruelling to the onlooker. We didn't write or profit about it unless your name happened to be called Helmut Grohmann. But he was a best-selling author anyway and people lapped up his so-called escapades because misplaced idealism still existed, with or without a figurehead like Hitler. Beware of what the future would bring, Albert often predicted. We never quite believed him, preferring instead to believe in weak leadership and shallow bonds with our neighbours just because we believed in European unity, a common market and united friendship.

But mostly our neighbours did not possess an entire shoreline like us thus making us truly independent. They had borders with other countries which had to be protected and manned. An Island should always stay an Island, no matter what. It made us great, and the people made us great, as well. No one would invade us in modern history. Full stop to that as well.

I continued to hold my dad to comfort him in his hour of need. Albert was an outwardly gentle man. He died peacefully if not annoyed at my ignorance of world affairs. I felt inadequate in his presence. Then I realised that in his lifeless heart was the safest hiding place, that he did things accordingly in a right way, not the coolest way as we did things today to prove a point. And he kept those feelings largely secret. He didn't need to prove anything to anyone except to himself and his heart. He had nerves of steel. And that was essential in our hour of need.

If my dad wasn't his, so what? He had succeeded at what he set out to do. Raise a child as his own, rightly or wrongly. No one should doubt his bravery as to the tasks he undertook. The British way! And Sheila should be commended to, not knowing who the real father was and choosing a life solely for the baby's future as she saw it. That took guts.

I saw a dead body. My dad wept and the staff cried as well. At an elderly age, it was not unexpected, just sad that another war veteran had passed away without telling their experience of the war but perhaps that is not important…it was too big and painful to illustrate the whole episode by word of mouth. That was left to the History Books and Orators of the period but was Albert ever asked for his opinion…no, because he would speak the truth and the truth stank. People were expendable in their millions in the name of so-called civilisation. And so they were cast aside to die en masse. The bigger picture (usually political) was all that mattered to the bigwigs.

Propaganda?

We all did it to secure victory and avoid humiliation. Just ask the obstinate Japanese when the Atom Bombs were dropped on their cities destroying everything in the blink of an eye. They surrendered immediately. Well, wouldn't you given the same circumstances of knowing what the enemy possessed? They did have a choice, even beforehand, but people were expendable in their millions and they knew this with their decision. Yet, still they were sacrificed despite what the Government expected. They were warned, and chose to ignore the threat. Completely unnecessary. They should have surrendered in the first place. Instead, they played with these innocent lives in their millions before surrendering. And exterminated them in the name of pride. Madness.

Today, we salute the fallen, but these same bigwig people who wallow in their sacrifice, killed them in the first place in the name of democracy. They just wear different expressions these days. This seems to placate the onlookers. Therefore, order is kept and sins hidden. It is the way of the world.

They weep in public with false tears.

My grandfather returned to Lincolnshire as a broken man to a starving family. He just got on with it. He didn't just think about it. His true feelings were locked away in his heart for safekeeping. Until his dying day, he was faithful to Sheila's true wishes and feelings. What did he say to me, defiant to the end: "he is not having your dad"? I believed those words. They were etched in my heart forever: the safest hiding place.

ooo

The cremation was in ten days' time, just enough time to tell everyone who wanted to attend the service. I phoned Sonia. I was desperate for news.

'How did it go?' I asked.

'You sound very down. What has happened?'

I told her the sad news.

'I'm truly sorry,' she said, 'when is the funeral?'

'In ten days' time. On the twenty-second in Sutton. He is being cremated, actually.'

'I'll be there…assuming I am being invited to attend.'

'Of course. It will be a small affair. Dad is clearing Albert's things up and notifying the last of the close friends and family as to the date. Anyway, how's things your end?'

Sonia paused and cleared her throat. I waited anxiously but thought I knew the response by her delay.

'We are barely talking—how do you say? Things "kicked off" when Isadora admitted her affair.'

'With Godfrey?' I interjected.

'With Godfrey Snapp…hell, no!'

I was horrified, 'Who then?' I gasped. 'It had to be Godfrey. He was crestfallen when we last spoke.'

'I knew about Godfrey. Anyway, when did you speak?' she asked.

'Last week.'

'When you were revisiting Venice?'

'Yes, we had a drink on my last night. I think he was lonely.'

'So he should be, but my father comes first…'

'Of course,' but my tone of voice betrayed me. Again.

'He was always faithful to her,' she snapped in response.

'But they have now stopped their affair.'

She sighed, 'Agreed. They stopped their affair.'

I was devastated by this apparent admission. She must have known about this, but kept quiet to protect people.

'However, I wish it was that simple,' she continued.

'Who then are we talking about?' I asked again.

'Jack.'

'Of Jack and Jill fame?' I said, stunned and feeling rather stupid.

'The very same. Jack Wiltshire. They have been having a secret liaison for several months.'

'So, whilst being a spy for the old man, he has been banging Isadora on the side.' I regretted saying the last bit. True, but, a little crude.

'Exactly!' Sonia announced.

I had got away with my comment.

'And counting the huge money on offer when your father finally passed away, and they married,' I added sarcastically.

'Hmm, and Jack has disappeared suddenly. Things were obviously getting too hot for him to handle.'

'Probably,' I countered, 'he went to America on business to set up a solo exhibition. Which was odd! What's wrong with a free email these days?'

'New York?' she prompted me.

'Think so. Why do you ask?'

'When did he go?'

'Recently.'

'That's funny, Isadora has just come back from there—on business apparently. As you said, what's wrong with an email? Cheaper than flying.'

ooo

I took the decision to go to Venice again. I smelled a rat. The Internet did not give me real insight and I needed facial expression which only face to face meetings truly gave me. I know there is Skype and Zoom but it is not the same.

Besides, dad had everything else under control. It was a waiting game until the cremation. I couldn't sit still. I closed the gallery.

So here I am again, poorer financially…trying my best to interfere with other people's problems. I can't solve all the issues but I somehow felt I owed Albert. I was up for any challenge that came my way. Besides, I wanted the truth. I've said that before. Talk about being a sucker for punishment. This saying described me perfectly. I was really trying, but failing.

I saw Sonia first. Her parents had separated. She had gone home to look after her dad's new fragility while his wife had moved out of the matrimonial house and was renting a large pad in the middle of the city temporarily. The local and national press were by now making a noise amid the gossip of a marriage breakdown. Nothing remained private for long in their region, as the front pages of the newspapers testified with their photographs plastered over them. How do you solve this? The reporters were having a field day, and probably sold out the morning issue. Such was the glamour and notoriety of this famous couple!

We met for coffee down an alleyway and sat alone. Thankfully.

'Tell me what happened, Sonia?' I whispered, although there was no one to overhear us. I was just being sensitive which was unusual for me. She just had that effect on me. Fool that I am.

'Dad met me at the airport as arranged and asked me what was up. I was flustered. During our chauffeur driven ride to the restaurant I blurted out what I knew from you and Albert and he began to cry, and so did I. He said he had been a bloody fool and we vowed to stick together and fight mum all the way if we had to.'

I was perplexed. 'With her affairs?'

'Well, Godfrey to begin with. The affair with Jack revealed itself later in the restaurant under our interrogation.'

'I didn't know about Jack…but we know his main motive. Money,' I said deeply. Somehow, I couldn't quite see them together, although she was beautiful and desirable and he was handsome…and now possibly filthy rich, especially when she became a widow in his reckoning and they married, and Helmut wasn't getting any younger anyway. So, any wait would be fairly short.

Sonia was distraught enough without me adding to her woes.

'What about his memoirs?' I dared to ask.

'What about them?'

'Well, you said he had been a bloody fool. Was he referring to his books and the falsehoods he made up or his marital complications…'

'You will have to ask him yourself… this evening.'

Damn, this was going to be harder than I thought. I was not a detective who would ask the correct questions. I just bumbled through and made an ass of things. Chaos seemed to follow me everywhere.

Chapter Eighteen

'Hello, Helmut,' I said, standing in the doorway to his kitchen with Sonia on my arm. She left us to it by retiring to her bedroom upstairs. I waited patiently for the two of us to be alone. He was drinking from a bottle of Malbec and raised his glass in my direction. Why not join the condemned in a so-called celebration or burial? I nodded and an empty glass was poured for me.

'Not sure if I would ever say this, but I am sorry to hear of your marriage problems,' I murmured.

'Have a seat and pull up,' he offered. I did and drank the wine nervously, hoping he would break the deathly silence first. He did.

'How are you, Martin?' He asked wearily.

'Not bad. And you?'

'Terrible. My world is falling apart, but you know this and you have been responsible for some of it.' He spoke like he had a bad taste in his mouth. He had a point with his words though. Was I that bad, or was this his way of passing the buck? I never encouraged any of this, did I? You might have a different story!'

'Thanks,' I muttered sarcastically under my breath. I felt like an executioner, but the architect must bear the main cost if things go wrong. And that was not going to be me, I thought adamantly. Helmut was the main architect in my book.

'This day would come,' I said. 'Tell me, how are you going to escape?'

'Ride the storm out with my wife beside me, hopefully. I couldn't fail my readers by revealing the truth of marital problems and then for her to take them on and try to grow the numbers again when I am long gone and I couldn't help manipulate them for her. That was not the plan, anyway. The empire is our empire. The alternative scenario doesn't bear thinking about. We have signed contracts with the publisher, and they are binding.'

'And now?' I asked, rather shocked by the 'alternative' scenario spoken by him. What did that entail, or was I being stupid again? I got my answer without prompting.

'Screw her for what she has done! I will bring the whole house down!'

'That is not a legacy of your choosing, Helmut.'

'Needs dictate. I did not anticipate this.'

That worried me. He had been drinking heavily, and probably wasn't aware of what he was saying.

'You will suffer…' I added.

He looked at me with triumph in his eyes.

'Hardly.'

'How did you get away with so many lies in your books? Did nobody check?'

'Readers are loyal, especially back home. No one really checked and we dismissed those who challenged a good story while the money grew and grew and I, to my eternal shame, chased after it. I was flattered by the fame and wanted more. It was easier to make up bits. Of course, I knew your dad and Albert were out there somewhere. We could deal with you at a distance if ever you made trouble. You were no real threat. Imagine my horror when you came over, so I put bloody Jack on it after our meeting before you arrived. Thought I could trust him…little did I know what he was up to…'

I intervened, 'I suspected Godfrey and to an extent, I was correct in my assumption, but he was elderly and famous in his own right and didn't need the hassle and was married anyway. He preferred no complications in his private life, if you get my meaning. He was no threat therefore. He was loyal to you, actually, despite sleeping with your wife, with your permission, I should hasten to add.'

'Who made him famous and rich and acceptable on the social map in the first place? He repaid me by having an affair with my wife.'

'With your permission to accommodate her wishes in the first place, I repeat!' I said. 'But he was harmless enough, and neither of you would live forever, even though you thought you would. The arrangement suited you both at the time, but Godfrey preferred to play the field. Who can blame him with so many nubile females arriving at his doorstep? Everybody dies, I'm sure you have heard the news of Albert's shocking passing?'

'Yes, I have. My daughter told me. I'm sorry. How many times have you been married?'

This was an odd question to ask. 'Three times, but you know that data from research…' I replied reluctantly.

'Indeed. Do you still have a love for them?'

How do you answer that truthfully? I was perplexed by this line of enquiry.

'Yes, my first wife I had a child with, the second I married too quickly and Lillian and I are separated and planning for divorce but I sort of still love them… they are part of my history. Why do you ask, by the way?'

'What is the common factor?'

It wasn't too hard to fathom. 'Me,' I said mutedly.

He repeated this phrase again.

'Me,' I re-emphasised. This was painful to admit.

'But you are not a bad man.'

'No. Just small errors on my part turned events against me—I only wanted to get married once.'

'I hate my wife,' Helmut concluded, with a certain nastiness in his voice.

'You say that now, it is understandable.'

'No, I hate her and how she has manipulated us. She will not get away with it.'

'Us?'

'Sonia in particular. Sonia's mother died when she was in late childbirth in Germany. I was devastated. Her name was Claudia. We were in love. Isadora was just starting out and I was making it big in my homeland as well as in Italy. Isadora interviewed me months later and we had… what do you call it?…we had a certain rapport, and the public lapped it up in spite of the tragedy that befell Claudia and I. The public almost demanded Isadora and I got married. The newspapers followed our story every day with our photos on the front pages.'

'Careers were almost made by then. Any public relationship was icing on the cake. Did you and her have an illicit affair?'

'We tried to keep it a secret because she was engaged to a TV actor at the time and we wanted to be fair.'

'So you manipulated him?'

'I was good at that sort of thing.'

'It takes two to tango,' I said.

'Yes, Isadora helped by stringing him along, and I put the knife in when we got serious in our relationship.'

'Were you reminded of Sheila in the first instance?'

'I suppose I was. Claudia also reminded me of Sheila. The resemblance was uncanny.'

'You could say that, I spotted a photo of her…was Sheila your first great love?' I asked nonchalantly.

'You could say that, but the war got in the way. You could argue that the conflict saved her. I offered her and the baby she carried a life she could not handle and could not fathom. How would I explain back home my love for a English girl? She would have been crucified! She was a country girl at heart, and I mainly a city boy. I was the foreigner, not her, in England.

So, she naturally chose England, after mulling things over. She was tormented by my offer though. The strange thing: it was my father who wanted to return home and join up with Hitler's vision to conquer Europe. That was beyond question to us as a family. How ironic that ill health failed his application to join the army and he only had one option: a desk job while I grabbed all of the early glory because I was the considered the perfect specimen. His loss, my gain, as they say.'

'Until the conflict all went pear-shaped.'

'Yes, you could say that as well! Before that moment, I moved up the ranks and used the experience to my advantage. Then we surrendered and I survived somehow, by the fumbled gunshot wound from Albert. He basically saved me. It rendered me incapable of shooting at the time. We suspected that the end was near and, like my comrades, were sick of things and this was a safety precaution in case we carried on.' He held up his disfigured hand to the light. 'It looks good for the book: my war wound,' he said triumphantly.

'So you even used that for to your advantage. What are you going to do next now we know Albert told the truth about your hand injury? You can be exposed.'

'I'm elderly and want to leave everything intact for Sonia, my only daughter from Claudia, my first wife. She deserves that. Isadora will get nothing.'

'How do you intend to do that?'

'Kill her. I'm used to that, being a child of the war. Then Sonia will inherit everything.'

'Aren't you forgetting someone?'

'Jack. He is on business in New York for me. I have influence over there. Right now he is locked up on a serious drug charge of carrying large amounts of heroin in the city—not to be just frowned upon by the police who searched him. He is therefore staring at a long jail sentence. My associates over there replanted the drugs on him and alerted the authorities. We won't be hearing from Jack for a very long time. If you try and dislodge that, I will deny talking to you. That just leaves my wife to take care of and I am seeing her shortly.'

'And you aim to kill her.'

'Yes. I'm an old man and will be dead soon anyway. What will they do with me anyway in the meantime? I am very elderly and will plead insanity or something like that in order to fight and win in the corrupt system that is in place. I will probably get let off. Remember, she also has enemies over here who resent her power on the network. It works both ways, of course, but I have numerous supporters in high places to help me in my quest for freedom, if I want it.' He stood calmly. 'Nice wine, why don't you finish the bottle. Have a toast on me. In the famous words of Oates, I may be some time.'

I stood as well. This tragic scenario spelt trouble. I had to read between the lines. 'I thought you were coming to London for a DNA test?' I asked.

'Ah, almost forgot. I have done it over here. No time like the present as our circumstances have changed dramatically since we last met. Conclusively, Albert is the father of Alec. I have a low sperm count. It is a miracle I fathered Sonia. Always have had a low sperm count, apparently. I had further tests. Proof is at my new doctor's…but he needs your cooperation before releasing it. My new doctor has a low profile at the moment, but that will change soon. Then, and only then, can you both reveal all, or you can let an old man die in peace. Your call.'

He handed me a piece of paper. 'Here is his contact number. I have also given him yours, so there is no confusion.'

'Don't ridicule me, Helmut. I have my own father to rely on to take the test.'

'Have you? Does he want to rock the boat? I doubt it he wants to take the chance, actually.'

'You just said you had a test!' I was angry with him.

'I did. But you need the proof and we have it. With your dad, you don't just need proof. Courage is also required.'

'Is Sonia your natural daughter?'

'I'm offended but thankfully, yes, and as I explained earlier to you, she came late in my life and Claudia, sadly, died giving birth. Age played a part in her death.'

'And the nephew in London?'

'We hardly communicate these days, but, yes, he is family as well.'

'Do they know what is going on?'

'Sonia, yes. My nephew, not yet. You can tell him one day. In the meantime, she is my daughter. I love her dearly, more than life itself. I want her to inherit everything. There is only one way to ensure this.'

'I could hold you hostage?'

He laughed hoarsely. 'For how long? You would deny Sonia all that is hers? I have changed my will, leaving her everything. I cannot risk my wife remarrying, which she will because of her young age, her fame, and of course, her basic needs and insatiable ambition. Therefore, I don't think I should fear your proposal, my friend. Rather, I need your silence. One of my offspring was equally hard to handle…'

'Dieter, your brother. Did you arrange his death?'

'Yes. We were not particularly close.'

This was chilling to hear. It meant nothing would get in the way of his need for public adulation. He craved this.

Helmut continued, 'He was a good art historian but, like you, he cleverly pieced together the past and persisted on questioning my judgment. He wouldn't let it go.'

'And ultimately, he paid with his life?'

'Sadly, yes. I did warn him. Several dissenting fans suffered the same fate.'

'You killed them?'

'I had them killed if they persisted in questioning me.'

'So Isadora is next?'

'Yes. Circumstances dictate it.'

'You are a cruel man.'

'A realistic man…'

'Am I in danger as well?'

'Of course. Did you think otherwise?'

'What do you want from me?'

'Walk away, would be a sensible option, and live another day and honour me.'

'And let the memoirs stand and allow the past to die with Albert?'

'Truth or fiction,' Helmut stated. 'You choose, but make sure fiction comes out on top. This way, we both win. You are free to marry Sonia in my view after both of you divorce and you can be rich together. That will give me great pleasure if you agree to my terms.'

'And keep Sonia ignorant of the facts?' I surmised. 'This needs thinking about seriously.' Sonia would take some convincing. No amount of wealth would persuade her, that I knew for certain. I might be a rascal, but she was not. We couldn't survive this way. It would destroy us. My mind was in turmoil.

When I turned to confront him, he was gone leaving me with his resolute daughter and a dilemma to solve with the devil. He had the easy bit to do, I reckoned. Then it suddenly hit me: he was going to kill himself tonight.

Chapter Nineteen

Actually, he gave me little choice but to be a bystander in the unfolding events.

I wasn't going to deny Sonia inheriting wealth over her half-mother getting it. Isadora would contest any will if she was alive and she was very beautiful and would use this to her advantage with courting publicity in the press.

Which she would get in these parts. All she had to do was keep a whiter than white image. Therefore, another Jack was always close by, hovering in the shadows, ready to pounce. She just had to keep them at arm's length. The past was too messy. Should Isadora be murdered though? It wasn't my decision. It could happen anytime, anywhere…natural death, that is.

It was Helmut's decision to be a killer as she had conspired against him and would pay the price for her treachery when he would have given her everything. On her own doorstep. I panicked. Should I keep quiet? I didn't know his new doctor, of course. Time was not on my side.

Then it hit me for a second time. The only way I would know him, would be Helmut's choice not to return from his meeting with Isadora. This examination by his doctor was private. Helmut would do the deed of getting rid of her and then commit suicide. The doctor then would reveal himself as a matter of course. So dual death was imminent. No, time was not on my side, but I had to act fast if I intended to stop this.

'Sonia! Sonia!' I shouted upstairs. 'What is your father's new doctor called?'

She came to her door. 'Gosh, I don't know, he had lots at his age as he was a hypochondriac by and large and then there was his plastic surgeon…the list goes on and on! Why?'

'Where is Isadora staying?' I asked frantically.

'Near the Rialto Bridge…'

'Where exactly?' My voice scared her.

'It is easier to show you. I'll get my coat.'

'Hurry.'

Then she turned to me with wide eyes. 'Where is daddy? He was here a minute ago.'

'We have no time to lose. Can you phone the police on our journey?'

'Is my dad in trouble?' she asked in puzzlement.

'He doesn't see it that way.'

She frantically followed me to the harbour with a mobile clasped in her hand.

ooo

We saw the bubbling wake of his speedboat in the distance. He was going fast and didn't care if he broke any speed limit that existed. He was on a mission.

'I've called the police and they will intercept him,' Sonia wailed as our vaporetto chugged along slowly in pursuit.

'What's he done?' Sonia asked in bewilderment this time.

'Plenty! It's what he wants to do that bothers me now,' I replied with my eye on the horizon as lights twinkled in the distance. We were getting close to the main island.

'Which is what exactly?'

I stared at her. 'Kill Isadora,' I stated coldly.

'No way,' she replied flippantly.

'Then himself.'

That remark focused her. Ashen-faced, she didn't speak again on the short journey over the water. Her tears spoke volumes instead.

ooo

The police swooped into her apartment and found it empty, I later learned.

Helmut was clever. He had met her at a prearranged time, near the Bridge of Sighs on the boardwalk near Doges Palace. It was busy with tourists as usual.

They had a short chat and she thought she was safe among admirers. How wrong can one person get? He shot her twice as she was approached by well-wishers who wanted an autograph as a lasting testament to her TV fame. That is what they got in return: being witness to her murder. One bullet hit her in the temple, the second shot to the heart made sure of his intention. He used his trusted army Luger to administer the bullets. He had over the years learned to use his other hand to perfect the fatal aim.

I and Sonia watched it unfold. He saw me as the water taxi pulled up amid the commotion. I now stood on the promenade, horror-struck. We locked eyes. Then Sonia rushed forward as he pulled the trigger once more and then his own

142

brain exploded over the promenade and his body toppled lifelessly into the lagoon.

Sonia stopped in her tracks and turned to me, sobbing.

'Why didn't you try and stop him?'

'I respected him in the only way I knew. If not now, he would have killed himself in the future.' Then I went and spoiled things with my next comment. 'Perhaps "respect" is a bit strong,' I added. Oops. I was in shock, not in charge of what spewed from my mouth.

'You call that respectful?' she screamed at me. The police arrived and retrieved his stricken body from the watery grave. Isadora's face was covered up, hiding her expression of horror to the gathering melee.

'I can only honour him as he requested me to,' I responded. It began to rain and the inquisitive crowd began to disperse. So did I. When things settled down, I would reveal the truth to her. I owed her that much. Now was not the time.

Sonia was mad at me, saying loudly: 'I have now lost both my parents.' She would at first grieve for her father. Any future between us would have to wait. In the meantime, we all got largely what we wanted. The heavens opened up. I liked Venice in the rain, as you know, and the wet pavements reflected our ghosts like no other place on this earth.

Albert, RIP. Your memory would not be tarnished.

I thought things through: You did the right thing, Albert, but you always knew that. You brought dad up the right way. It was other people who doubted you, including me; shame on all of us. I felt small. And tarnished.

But Sonia would get her wealth in the future without interruption, Jack was arrested abroad, Isadora killed, Helmut also dead, his will revised, Albert deceased and Godfrey had the city to himself without interference which he always wanted. An artist in his own right.

Helmut used an unknown doctor for his examination, I later learned, who would then become very well known in celebrity circles when he revealed himself to the public with his findings.

Me? I am just an ordinary art dealer from London who came to Venice on business and met the wrong companion, which opened up a whole can of worms that my family did not need. I could now go back to my hole in London and lick my wounds and discuss matters with my dad. Others could not discuss matters now, sadly.

At the airport, Lillian rang me and we talked (correction: I listened again) and I dreaded my life back home. But the facts had to be faced head-on. There was no escape for me. I had to face the music.

Then a familiar voice interrupted me.

'Coming or going?' Jill asked.

What did I have to lose? I was on my own.

'Going,' I said, laughing. 'What brought you back to Venice?'

'It is my temporary home. Shall we check the ticket situation?'

'Yes,' I replied, taking her arm. We had unfinished business, lots to do and talk about and she still had the best arse around (well, the best around here at this precise moment). Beggars can't be choosers. And I felt like a beggar. Helmut was right, any story needed a slight detour for it to lure the fans in and demand more. He was a master at storytelling, we were the simple puppets who wanted more from his masterly pen.

Maybe I would write his final days, but who would believe me or even want the truth to maybe spoil things.

'Well?' I said to Jill.

She returned from a desk, beaming from ear to ear. It told a story without the need for words.

'Did you meet with Sonia in London?' She enquired.

'I did. She is just a friend.'

'Will you be seeing her again in London?'

'Fifty-fifty,' I announced.

'I'll take those odds,' she beamed.

'Where did you suddenly go?' I asked her in a bemused fashion.

'Oh, here and there, but with this body I don't have to worry.'

I then thought of my empty house and needed someone there with me.

'Let's go,' she remarked, 'and have some fun.'

'Don't you yearn to see Jack?' I asked reasonably.

'Jack? He's history…'

Right now, I figured, we were all consigned to history.

I followed, licking my lips. A rollercoaster beckoned. That's how I survived. A leopard never changes its spots.

Don't try this at home, folks!

Sonia would speak to me again, eventually. When, though? Maybe six months, a year perhaps, two years? Let her calm down! Then, maybe sooner for all I knew. Jill would move on fairly quickly.

I shall come to Venice again. It has the intrigue I crave for. I like meeting broken people. I am drawn to unusual places. My past is settled. I'm English by nature. My personal future is less certain in marriage. I'll go with the flow, and in the meantime 'have some fun'. I deserve that, don't you agree? I told you not to follow me. After all, I am just a geezer telling a story.

Believe it or not, the choice is yours depending on my viewpoint and yours, of course. History never tells it accurately or correctly. I had to find mine the hard way, I learned that. But here I am, bruised and battered, but content at last, I think.

Are you happy with your lot?

The End

Milton Keynes UK
Ingram Content Group UK Ltd.
UKHW022032181123
432826UK00005B/75